SERENITY

BY

DANIEL DUKE

Published by: Daniel Linden Duke

ISBN: 978-1-964452-34-0 (sc)
ISBN: 978-1-964452-33-3 (eb)
ISBN: 978-1-964452-35-7 (hb)

Library of Congress Control Number: 2024925246

Printed in the United States of America

OTHER NOVELS BY THE AUTHOR

MAN CAMP

RIVER OF DREAMS

PURSUIT OF HAPPINESS

DEDICATION

TO A LOVING HEART AND A JOYFUL SPIRIT,
MY DAUGHTER, DEVAN ELENA COOPER.

CHAPTER 1

SATURDAY, SEPTEMBER 10, 2022

Sara Castle normally looked forward to Saturday coffee and pastry with her daughter, Marie. Parker, Marie's husband, stayed home with four-year-old Marcus so that Sara and Marie could enjoy an hour or so without having to keep the rambunctious youngster entertained. These occasions took on special significance the longer the Pandemic wore on because Sara's social life had dried up faster than a drought-stricken California lawn.

This particular Saturday, however, found Sara less than enthusiastic about Marie's arrival. Ever since Marcus's birth, Marie had embraced mothering in a big way. Mothering her new son and her husband failed to quench Marie's desire for care-giving. She insisted on mothering her mother as well. There were even times lately when mothering Sara gave way to straight-out bossiness and excessive unsolicited advice.

To be fair, Sara had needed mothering in the immediate aftermath of the tragic, unexpected death of David, her husband of thirty years. She marveled at Marie's ability, so soon after her son's birth, to deal with the myriad challenges of first-time motherhood, cope with the loss of her father, and comfort her grieving mother. As far as Sara was concerned, the girl had inherited her father's talent for time management and multi-tasking.

Generally, Sara managed time pretty well herself with one exception. Almost anything related to the visual arts attracted her and therefore had the potential to distract her. Sara could pass an art gallery window after visiting a cheese shop, stop to admire a new painting, study the artist's use of color and light for thirty minutes or so, and in the process earn a parking ticket and a bag of melted cheese.

When art was not involved, however, she diligently focused on the things that needed her attention, ranging from weekly babysitting for young Marcus to managing the household expenses and preparing meals. On the few occasions when her budget was out of whack, it probably resulted from an impulsive purchase of an intriguing painting or photograph.

Ever since Sara decided to go ahead with the second honeymoon cruise that David had booked before his accident, Marie expressed her disapproval. Each Saturday during her visit with Sara she offered a new reason why the trip was a bad idea. Cruising around the eastern Mediterranean would be dangerous because Greece was threatening military action against Turkey over disputed territory. Cruise ships could be breeding grounds for all kinds of viruses. Older women traveling alone were prime targets for scam artists and predatory males.

Sara conceded that these reasons possessed some validity, but they didn't bother her as much as Marie's most recent argument. Last Saturday she warned that going on the second honeymoon cruise could produce a painful longing that might never be resolved. David was gone, and that was that. Instead of producing a sense of closure, the cruise was more likely to re-open a gaping wound.

Marie's latest admonition had merit, Sara acknowledged, but she was not one of those people who regarded life as an unending quest for pain avoidance. Maybe it was the artist in her, for Sara valued sadness. Sorrow helped to keep things in perspective and, under the right circumstances, could inspire creativity.

Marie failed to wrap her head around the notion that sadness could be beneficial. She became upset when her dire warnings failed to change her mother's decision to travel. Marie, like her father, was accustomed to getting her own way. The fact that Sara calmly listened to her arguments without accepting them agitated Marie.

With the notable exception of David's unexpected death, very little unnerved Sara. Her hippie parents, Sara believed, must have possessed a sixth sense regarding their newborn daughter's character because they named her Serenity. Her name, predictably, became a source of embarrassment for Serenity Sunshine Stevens in high school. She initially shortened her name to Serena. By the time she graduated from the University of Virginia, Serena had been reduced to Sara.

In a few minutes Marie would arrive and make a last-ditch plea for Sara to stay home, a plea that once again would be rejected. The cruise was paid for, and the cruise line had postponed it twice already due to Pandemic-related restrictions. The world was re-opening now, and the cruise line notified customers that no refunds would be offered to those who declined to sail next week. Sara had no intention of squandering an expensive adventure. David had worked hard to pay for the cruise. To back out now would be irresponsible. If Sara had one quality that rivaled her calmness, it was a sense of responsibility.

Sara would try one last time to explain to Marie that the cruise was scheduled to visit some places where she and David had gone on their original honeymoon, a backpacking, train-hopping journey across southwestern Europe. After three decades, memories of that trip were fading. No longer were there photographs of the honeymoon to help revive those memories. An attic fire took care of the album she painstakingly put together after returning. Sara now desired to stand in places where she and David once stood and re-imagine what their time together had been like. A self-styled visual thinker, Sara needed to be on location to be inspired.

There was one additional motivation for Sara's upcoming trip, but she would not attempt to explain it to Marie. Sara still felt considerable guilt over David's death, despite efforts by family and friends to convince her that his accident was not her fault.

As Sara saw it, if she had not insisted on playing pickleball that Sunday three years earlier, she would not have taken a hard fall and fractured her hip just weeks before she and David planned to take a combined business trip and short vacation to South Carolina and Florida. Unable to accompany her husband because of post-surgical restrictions related to her hip replacement, Sara remained at home with Marie and Marcus while David completed the business portion of the trip in South Carolina. Had Sara been able to go along, she and David would have driven to Tampa after he finished meetings with potential donors for the University of Virginia's capital campaign. Instead, David started driving back to Charlottesville. Just before reaching the interstate highway, he was T-boned at an intersection by a speeding trucker who ignored the traffic signal. David died at the scene.

Sara never had an opportunity to say goodbye. To make matters worse, Marie had to go to South Carolina to recognize the body before it could be released and sent back home. Marie's husband, Parker, stayed with Sara and Marcus during Marie's absence.

Sara might have been serene by nature, but her serenity was no match for the guilt that haunted her. In some strange way that she herself didn't fully understand, completing the second honeymoon cruise offered Sara a chance to put David's death and her associated guilt behind her. She was completing what she and David had set out to do. He would be with her, in her heart if not by her side.

As for what waited for Sara at the end of the cruise, several possibilities occurred to her, but she had no intention of sharing them with Marie or Randy, her son. Unlike Marie, Randy encouraged his mother to go on the cruise. Three years older than his sister, Randy believed travel to be therapeutic. As a pilot for United Airlines, he loved exploring new places and meeting new people. Randy was as much a reflection of his mother as Marie was of her father.

Marie uncharacteristically arrived fifteen minutes late for coffee. Even more unusual was the news she brought. Rather than delivering the anticipated sermon on the dangers of cruising the Mediterranean, Marie announced that Parker had been offered a promotion if he agreed to move to the head office in Charlotte. The promotion came with a hefty raise in salary, enough to permit Marie to look for a bigger home. A bigger home, in turn, would enable Marie and Parker to have another child.

Sara sat in stunned silence as Marie detailed her plans. The only things mitigating the terrible loneliness Sara felt following David's death were her regular get-togethers with Marie, Parker, and Marcus along with babysitting Marcus three days a week. Now, if she chose to return to Charlottesville, there would be even more empty time to fill. The friendships she and David shared already had evaporated during the Pandemic's early days. Initiative was required to make new friends, and it was in short supply for Sara.

When Marie gave Sara a puzzled look and asked why she hadn't responded to her exciting news, Sara feigned a smile and offered muted congratulations, then added she was glad they weren't moving as far as Denver, where Randy now lived. Marie acknowledged that Marcus would miss Nana.

Marie continued talking about the impending move for an hour, then abruptly announced she needed to return home and contact realtors in Charlotte. Compounding the surprise news of the family's departure was Marie's comment as she rose to leave. She apparently now believed that going on the second honeymoon cruise was a good idea. Her parting words disoriented Sara. "Maybe you'll meet a handsome widower when you're in Europe. The time for grieving over Dad is over."

Sara didn't know what to say. She remained seated, sipping her coffee and trying to process all the thoughts circulating in her head. Did it still make sense to try and make a go of it in Charlottesville when her family was elsewhere? Once upon a time, the prospect of a diminished social life would not have been upsetting. That was back in the days when Sara was an aspiring artist. Solitude, not socializing, was what mattered. All of that changed, of course, when she met David. He loved meeting people. His social skills, in fact, had been keys to his success as a development officer raising money for higher education institutions.

Prior to marrying, Sara derived meaning from artistic expression and the search for inspiration. After falling in love with David, her sources of meaning gradually shifted. When Randy and Marie were born, being needed displaced creativity as Sara's wellspring of gratification. That continued when she abandoned her plan to return to graduate school and took a teaching job to help her growing family make ends meet. Later it was her mother who needed care after she was diagnosed with Alzheimer's disease. Who would need her now that Marie, Parker, and Marcus were moving to Charlotte and unmarried Randy was living in Denver?

The second honeymoon cruise now seemed to constitute more of an ending than Sara had expected, the epilogue to a story that started thirty years earlier. Would a new story begin when she stepped off the plane at Dulles International Airport in several weeks? One possibility, of course, was that her story could conclude with the second honeymoon. Suicide, after all, is the ultimate form of self-expression. Sara thought about Vincent Van Gogh's finale. He bid adieu with a brilliant painting of a path disappearing into a wheatfield below a darkening sky filled with crows and then took his life.

To begin a new story upon her return from the cruise would require enormous energy. "At fifty-five, do I have the wherewithal to launch a new life?" Sara asked herself. "I did decide to undertake the cruise alone. That's a good sign." Sara was thankful for David's life insurance, the settlement from his accident, and the funds he so wisely invested. "At least money won't be an issue if I decide to write a new chapter."

Sara abruptly stopped mulling over future options and resorted to what she always did when confronted by existential complexities. She chose to re-focus on practical matters. Tomorrow she would drive to Dulles and catch a plane to Istanbul. Her suitcase was only half-packed. She now needed to get on-line and find out the weather forecast for Turkey and the eastern Mediterranean. Then she could complete her packing. Mostly casual, comfortable items plus a fashionable outfit or two, she decided.

After learning that the weather was expected to be unseasonably hot, Sara went to finish packing in the spare bedroom where she occasionally slept when David snored too loudly. Passing a full-length mirror, she stopped for a quick check. Her close-cropped brown hair revealed touches of gray here and there, but not enough to suggest rapidly advancing age. Her chin line was well-defined, not too fleshy. The blue of her eyes was paler than in years past, but only slightly. As for her body, it was a few pounds heavier than thirty years ago, but her dress size was still a six, and her breasts were shapely, not sagging. Years of daily workouts and neighborhood walks definitely had been beneficial.

For a fleeting moment, Sara permitted herself to wonder whether Marie's "handsome widower" would find her desirable. She quickly reminded herself, however, that her journey's purpose was not to find a new mate, but to appreciate the man she loved and come to terms with what might lie ahead for her. With the right prompts, Sara could be truly gifted when it came to visualizing past experiences. As for envisioning the future, however, her canvas was blank.

CHAPTER 2

Sara's ten-hour Turkish Airlines flight was scheduled to land at Istanbul's Ataturk International Airport around eight in the morning. Despite ordering three mini-bottles of whiskey, her mind was too active to permit sleep on the plane.

She thought about her son, Randy, and what his life as a commercial airline pilot must be like. He had seen a good portion of the United States and recently became eligible for international flights. Both of Sara's parents had been scared of flying. Logan, her father, flew under duress when the film company he worked for required filming on location, but he made certain he traveled with anti-anxiety medication. Her mother, Gwen, refused to fly under any circumstances. When asked her reason, she insisted that flying disrupted the harmony of the universe, but in truth she was frightened of heights. Why her parents' fear of flying hadn't rubbed off on Sara remained a much-debated family mystery.

Eventually Sara pulled out her cruise itinerary and reviewed the ports of call. The Argonaut, her ship, departed from Istanbul on Wednesday, September 14, and sailed to Kavala on the northeast coast of Greece. Sara signed up for an excursion from Kavala to Xanthi. She purposely chose not to commit to any additional excursions sponsored by Wanderlust, the cruise line, because she hoped to meet another woman traveling alone. The two of them then could share some private tours along the way. Otherwise, Sara planned to go on her own to places that she and David had visited on their honeymoon.

On the third day of the cruise, the Argonaut docked at the Greek port of Volos. Sara read that the cluster of monasteries in Meteora was a "must see" destination. The island of Santorini came next, followed by a day at sea on the way to Taormina, Sicily. Ports five through ten were all places that Sara and David visited. They included Sorrento, Rome, Livorno, Marseille, Barcelona, and Almeria. Cadiz on the southern coast of Spain was scheduled for day thirteen, then on to Lisbon and disembarkation.

It had been decades since Sara felt as unfettered as she now did. She was even open to leaving the cruise at some point if she discovered a charming place that beckoned to her. David would have understood. Thanks to Marie's surprise announcement, there was no reason for Sara to rush back to Charlottesville. Why get caught up in helping Marie pack up her household?

In her youth Sara often became impatient with herself for not accomplishing more. Sometimes she blamed her laid back parents for not holding her to higher expectations or pushing her more. The same could not be said for David's parents. Both were highly educated and insistent on David excelling in everything he undertook.

In the midst of Sara's musings about her life, the captain announced that the plane would be landing soon. Make sure seatbelts were fastened and tray tables stowed. Hand any trash items to the flight attendants. Remain seated until the plane reached the gate and the seat belt sign was turned off. For a fleeting moment, a devilish little voice in Sara's head urged her to disobey the instructions.

Once she deplaned, cleared the passport checkpoint, grabbed her luggage, and passed through customs, Sara hailed a taxi and headed into Istanbul to the Hotel Eurasia. Three things impressed her during the frenetic ride: Istanbul's immense size, the heavy volume of traffic, and the network of tunnels beneath the metropolis. Sara visualized an enormous ant colony.

The Hotel Eurasia rose twenty-five stories over a tree-covered section of Istanbul near the Bosphorus. A slender young valet greeted Sara and carted her luggage into the hotel while she paid the taxi driver. She lined up at the registration desk along with a dozen other individuals. After waiting ten minutes for her turn, Sara angrily watched an elderly man in a wheelchair maneuver in front of her. Regardless of his disability, she found the action rude. Would it have been so hard to ask her if he could go ahead? Sara gladly would have consented. She was about to confront the man when an attractive young woman rushed up to her and apologized profusely for her father's discourteous conduct.

Spotting the nametag on Sara's suitcase, the woman commented, "You have a beautiful name. I've never met anyone named Serenity."

"Everyone calls me Sara. And you are?"

"I'm Pastel Greene. Perhaps you've heard of my father, Brendan Greene." She gestured toward the man in the wheelchair.

"The writer?" Sara sounded surprised. She decided not to mention her dislike of the one book of Greene's that she had read. Having completed the registration process, Brendan Greene instructed his daughter to assist him in getting settled. Sara never got a chance to comment on how much she liked Pastel's name.

After registering and receiving her room key, Sara stopped by the concierge desk to book a tour of Istanbul for the following day. She purposely arrived two days early so she could see some of the legendary bi-continental city before boarding the Argonaut. After several attempts to find an English-speaker, a tour guide was found. He asked Sara to wear comfortable shoes and meet him in the lobby at nine o'clock. Before leaving the concierge, she acquired a map of the city.

The view from Sara's twentieth floor room offered a panorama of the Bosphorus and the Asian side of Istanbul. After gazing at the teeming city and busy waterway below for several minutes, Sara felt a pang of regret that David never got the chance to see what she was seeing. She unpacked her suitcase in a melancholy mood, then told herself to cheer up and take advantage of her time in Istanbul. Though she had gotten little rest on the plane, Sara felt surprisingly awake and ready to stretch her legs. The map indicated that Taksim Square was close to the hotel.

Taksim Square was a carnival of activity. Tourists, vendors, and local families intermingled as uniformed soldiers with weapons patrolled the fringes of the square. The sight of soldiers did not alarm Sara. She reasoned that security concerns were one of the constants for twenty-first century travelers. David used to say that the time to worry was when no security personnel were visible. In the center of the square stood the impressive Republic Monument with its cast of Turkish heroes led by Kemal Mustapha Ataturk, the nation's George Washington. Sara was fascinated by the seagulls competing for space on the monument.

When she completed a walk around Taksim Square, Sara decided to stroll along Istiklal Caddesi, Istanbul's main pedestrian boulevard. The farther she walked, the denser became the foot traffic. Individuals on bicycles tried to weave their way through the crush of humanity. Ten minutes of trying to dodge bikes and avoid bumping into people was enough for Sara. Weary and worried about purse snatchers, she reversed course and headed back to the relative calm of her hotel.

By the time she reached Hotel Eurasia, Sara's growling stomach reminded her she hadn't eaten in a long time. The adventuresome Sara considered exploring a nearby neighborhood in search of an authentic Turkish dinner, but the practical Sara vetoed that option in favor of taking the elevator to the twenty-fifth floor for dinner and glimpses of Istanbul as it transitioned from daytime hustle to evening charm.

When Sara exited the elevator and entered the hotel restaurant, a stunning young woman with almond-shaped eyes and shoulder-length black hair greeted her and asked if she wished to sit by one of the enormous windows overlooking the city.

"Why wouldn't I?" Sara responded enthusiastically.

The woman took a moment to process Sara's remark, then answered, "Some of our guests feel uncomfortable being so high."

Sara was struck by the hostess's beauty and wondered if she might also be a model. When they reached the table, Sara asked about the view. The hostess explained that the body of water in the distance was called the Golden Horn. Along its shoreline were some of Istanbul's oldest neighborhoods and business districts. The tall structure that rose above most of the older buildings, she noted, was the Galata Tower, built long ago by the Italians. When Sara pulled out her camera, the hostess offered to take her picture with the Galata Tower in the background.

Within seconds of being seated, a server arrived and asked

Sara if she preferred sparkling or still water. "Still water is fine, but what I really want is a glass of white wine. Can you recommend a Turkish wine that I can try?"

"Turkey grows wonderful grapes, madam. I will bring you two to try."

After the server left, Sara wondered if she should have requested the sparkling water. When she used to travel with David, he always checked beforehand to determine whether the local water was safe to drink.

Sara was very glad she chose to eat at the hotel. The friendliness of the staff was impressive and made her feel special. Considerable time had passed since she felt that way. Surveying the city as its evening lights began to dot the landscape, Sara believed that David would have enjoyed Istanbul's cosmopolitan ambiance and rich mixture of diverse cultures. She recalled how he loved to engage total strangers in conversation in order to learn more about the place he was visiting. He would have spoken to both the hostess and the server, finding out their names, where they were from, and what they liked about Istanbul. As one of his former girlfriends told Sara, "David could charm the habit off a nun."

"Is that you, Serenity?" The voice startled her. Who knew her in Istanbul?

Swiveling around in her seat, Sara found Pastel Greene standing beside a nearby table with the hostess. "Do you mind if I join you?"

"Will your father be coming as well?"

"Don't worry. He's busy working on the draft of his new book. He ordered room service."

"I'd love the company, Pastel. You caught me admiring this magnificent view."

Pastel looked past Sara at the city below. As she did, Sara studied her face. Pastel's short, dark hair, dark eyes, and contrasting fair skin reminded her of John Singer Sargent's portrait of Lady Agnew of Lochnaw. Pastel, however, did not exude the independence and enigmatic persona of Lady Agnew.

The server appeared with two local wines for Sara and Pastel to try. Both women noted the wines were fruity, but with a dry finish. Sara ordered a bottle of the first wine, but warned the server that they eventually might want a bottle of the second wine as well.

"I meant to tell you when we were in the registration line that I love your name," Sara exclaimed. "Is it a family name?"

"My parents agreed that, if I were a boy, Dad would choose my name."

"So, your mother named you?"

"She's an artist. I bet you could have guessed," Pastel laughed. "If I'd been a boy, Dad would have chosen Norman, after Norman Mailer."

"Thank goodness you turned out to be a girl," Sara replied. "Given your father's Irish name, I would have thought he'd call you Kelly Greene if you were a boy."

Pastel smiled. "Anything would be better than Pastel. My mother must have had some intuition regarding my character when I was born. There's nothing vividly colorful about me."

"I disagree," Sara responded emphatically. "In my opinion, pastels are the warm and endearing colors of springtime when life is renewed following winter's bleakness."

"Sounds like you're an artist, too," Pastel commented.

"That's a long and somewhat sad story, I'm afraid. Let's just say I never became the artist I wanted to be because of interruptions. I'm sure you've watched those romcoms where every time the would-be lovers try to kiss or make love, they're interrupted by a phone call or a door bell or an unexpected emergency. That's my life in a nutshell, one interruption after another. Every time I built up a head of steam to press forward with my art work, something else came up to derail my plans."

"Sounds dreadful."

"Don't get me wrong. My husband and I had a wonderful life together with two successful children to show for it."

Pastel wrinkled her brow. "That's a sore subject for me. I'm twenty-seven years old and still searching for what I want to be. I'm sure I'm a big disappointment to my parents."

"Are you a disappointment to yourself?"

"Disappointment stalks me like a jilted lover."

Sara was going to comment that Pastel did not answer her question, but the server arrived with menus, and the women took a few minutes to review the offerings and make inquiries. Sara eventually chose a seafood salad with scallops and calamari, while Pastel opted for shish kabob. The server recommended the red pepper hummus as an appetizer.

Pastel asked about Sara's husband, noting that she spoke of him in the past tense. When Sara explained why David did not accompany her on what was supposed to be their second honeymoon cruise, Pastel apologized for bringing up a sensitive subject. Sara started to tell Pastel that she felt, in some spiritual way, that David actually was with her on the trip, but she changed her mind and instead asked why Pastel and her father were visiting Istanbul.

"We're on a cruise, too," she replied. "Dad was invited to be the Writer-in-Residence on the Argonaut. All expenses paid. We will sail the day after tomorrow."

"What a small world. I'm on the same ship."

Pastel flashed a broad smile. "I'm so glad. At least I'll know one person on board besides my father."

Sara refilled their wine glasses. "Say, I know it's short notice, but would you like to take a tour of Istanbul with me tomorrow. I've hired a guide."

"I'd love to. Dad will be working on presentations for the cruise. Besides, he hates guided tours. Listening to others is not his forte."

"When you're back home, what do you do to keep occupied?" Sara asked. "According to my father, I'm always on my cell phone. He told folks back home that he invited me to join him on the cruise so I wouldn't waste all of my time on social media, but I think the real reason was that he felt sorry for me." Pastel spread hummus on a piece of pita bread. "All of my sorority sisters have gone to Europe except me. I've been helping Dad by word processing his manuscripts. He still writes on a typewriter, if you can believe it."

"Do you edit his work as well?"

"Are you joking? He believes that every word he types has been inspired by the Gods. Just between us girls, though, he does make mistakes now and then."

Sara and Pastel spent the next hour sharing life experiences, drinking wine, and eating dinner. Pastel excused herself at eight thirty, saying that she promised to return by then to see if her father needed anything before going to bed. Sara reminded her to wear comfortable shoes for the tour and meet her in the hotel lobby a little before nine in the morning.

As she sipped the last of the wine, Sara surveyed the undulating carpet of lights below, extending as far as the eye could see. For a while, she thought about how the view, or at least a portion of it, might be captured on canvas. Then she reflected on Pastel and how different from Marie she was. Marie exuded confidence and clarity. She knew who she was and what she needed to do. Pastel, on the other hand, seemed lost and a little sad. Being raised by two high achievers had to be challenging. Sara imagined that Pastel's mother rarely tucked her into bed as a child or took an active interest in the youngster's hopes and dreams. She looked forward to getting to know Pastel. For a moment, she even forgot why she had come to Istanbul.

CHAPTER 3

TUESDAY, SEPTEMBER 13, 2022

Sara and Pastel met up in the Hotel Eurasia lobby a few minutes before nine. Pastel remarked that she was thankful to have packed shorts because the temperature was expected to reach ninety degrees. Sara wore a loose-fitting dress. In case they visited air-conditioned buildings, she carried a light sweater in her travel purse. The pair had just begun to discuss some of the landmarks they hoped to see when a husky and well-tanned middle-aged man who hadn't shaved in several days walked up and asked if one of the women was Sara Castle.

"I'm Sara Castle, and this young woman is Pastel Greene. She'll be joining us on the tour, if you don't mind."

"Why would Mehmet mind escorting two beautiful women instead of one?" He spoke rapidly with a distinct accent.

Sara and Pastel looked at each other knowingly. Sara was glad she had a companion.

Mehmet explained that he was named after one of the Ottoman Empire's most illustrious sultans.

"You mean you weren't named after Doctor Oz?" Pastel asked with a grin.

Mehmet had heard of the Turkish-American television personality. "Don't you think I'm more handsome?" he replied.

Sara began to think this guy might be a problem, but her hotel account already had been charged for the tour. What did it matter, anyway? She'd endured obnoxious men before. They typically turn out to be all talk.

As they left the hotel, Mehmet explained that they would catch a taxi and head to Istanbul's most historic district. He pointed out their destination on his pocket map. Following a harrowing ride better suited to an amusement park, the trio was dropped off near a mosque surrounded by scaffolding.

"My tours always begin at the Blue Mosque," Mehmet informed his companions. "Please note that there are six minarets, not the usual four. Unfortunately, repairs are currently underway, so it will be impossible for you to appreciate the delicate beauty and craftsmanship of the mosque."

Sara felt like saying, "Then why did you bring us here?"

Mehmet guided Sara and Pastel to a line of visitors entering the building and said he would wait for them near the exit. Once inside, everyone removed their shoes and shuffled into the main prayer room. Sara was sorry she had not brought a scarf, since most of the women visitors covered their heads out of respect. Views of the exquisitely detailed ceiling were obscured by construction draperies and scaffolding.

As they searched for their shoes before leaving, Sara advised Pastel not to say anything that Mehmet might interpret as flirty. Pastel said she had a canister of mace in her backpack "just in case." Both women expressed their disappointment about the Blue Mosque visit to Mehmet, who was smoking a cigarette near the exit. He assured them that the next stop would not be disappointing and gestured across an open expanse toward the Hagia Sophia, the largest mosque in the world.

Along the pedestrian concourse connecting the two mosques, Mehmet reached out to hold Sara's hand. She didn't mind because the pavement was uneven and she worried about tripping. The sensation of holding a man's hand reminded her of David. Early in their relationship they held hands a lot, but eventually David, whose pace was faster than Sara's, tended to walk ahead. She couldn't recall the last time they walked hand-in-hand.

When the threesome reached the enormous Hagia Sophia, a long line of visitors was snaking around the building. Mehmet explained that the mosque had been built in 360 A.D. as an Orthodox church. When the Ottomans captured Constantinople, it was converted to a mosque. Later the mosque became a museum. Recently, though, Turkey's president decided Hagia Sophia should revert to being a mosque.

Without warning, Mehmet, who already held Sara's hand, grabbed Pastel's hand and pulled the two women ahead of the waiting line. He apologized for startling them, then pointed to a side entrance that had just opened for visitors. Once again, he planned to wait outside while the pair admired the magnificent interior of the mosque.

"That was really creepy", Pastel said once they were out of earshot of Mehmet. "I don't like being grabbed that way."

"I've got an idea," Sara replied. "Let's you and me hold hands when we leave. Maybe that'll discourage him."

Pastel liked Sara's suggestion. Sara got the impression that Pastel felt uncomfortable, not only around Mehmet, but probably men in general. She was feeling motherly toward her young companion. Years had passed since there were similar feelings with Marie. Even as an adolescent, Marie had been mature beyond her years. By the time she finished high school, Marie was an independent woman making major life decisions on her own.

After removing their shoes and placing them in a designated area along with hundreds of other pairs of shoes, the women expressed the hope they would be able to find them later. Once they entered the main section of the mosque, Sara spent so much time gazing at the massive main dome that her neck started to hurt. Pastel meanwhile was fixated on the throngs of people inside the mosque. Sara finally asked if large crowds made her nervous, and she admitted being concerned. Very few visitors wore masks.

When Sara and Pastel met up with Mehmet, this time holding hands, he announced that the Topkapi Palace was the next stop, followed by an authentic Turkish lunch on Istanbul's Asian side. The Ottoman palace was a short walk from Hagia Sophia. Mehmet explained that the palace was too vast to see in its entirety. He winked and recommended focusing on the seraglio where the sultan's harem lived.

When the women reached the seraglio, a docent provided information about the inhabitants who once called the quarters home. Many were Christians captured during the Ottoman conquest of the

Balkans. As concubines, their primary responsibility was to provide the sultan with male heirs. When a woman gave birth to a male child, her duty was fulfilled. No further children were expected of her.

What Sara and Pastel found especially interesting was the influence a concubine could gain by being the mother of a male child. The child became a prince, one of many half-brothers. At a relatively young age each prince along with his mother was dispatched to some outpost of the Ottoman Empire. There the prince served as the titular head of government. The real power, however, often was wielded by the prince's mother. Mothers needed to be on guard in case a rival prince's mother tried to have their sons assassinated, thereby eliminating potential rivals when the sultan died and a prince had to be elevated to that exalted position.

The docent's fascinating remarks got Sara thinking about her grandson. She joked with Pastel that, if her daughter Marie had been an Ottoman concubine, Marcus would have certainly become the next sultan.

By noon, Sara and Pastel were tired of touring the palace and very hungry. They found Mehmet smoking outside the gate to the palace and chatting with several other tour guides. He asked Sara if she would have enjoyed being a concubine at Topkapi Palace. "Only if you were the eunuch, Mehmet," she replied.

The threesome boarded a rapid transit train and sped across the Bosphorus, eventually disembarking at a lovely shopping area full of cafes and interesting stores. Mehmet guided Sara and Pastel to a restaurant called Kabob Krazy and introduced them to the owner, a large man with a very bushy mustache and wearing a red beret. Sara assumed he and Mehmet were either friends or business associates. Mehmet wished the women a pleasant lunch and said he'd return at one thirty. After a hectic morning with, according to Pastel's exercise watch, over four miles of walking, a leisurely lunch sounded perfect.

The women agreed to share a sampler plate of Turkish dishes and a bottle of local chardonnay. While they waited for their order, Sara commented on how the historic characters they were learning about had interesting descriptors following their names. Selim the Grim. Suleyman the Magnificent. Vlad the Impaler. Sara asked Pastel what descriptor she would append to her name.

"Pastel the Timid," she replied.

When Sara asked her why, Pastel revealed that she had trouble speaking up for herself. To illustrate, she told a story about her parents. One day before she left for college, her father requested that she join him in his study. After chatting for a while, he asked Pastel what she wanted to focus on at Yale. When she expressed her interest in becoming a writer, he grew visibly upset and insisted she pursue another career. Writing for a living, he said, would condemn her to a life of disappointment, loneliness, and frustration. Instead of telling her father that becoming a writer was her choice to make, she accepted his advice and planned to major in anthropology. Then she shared her plans with her mother, who told her there were no jobs in anthropology and it would be smarter to major in sociology. Once again, Pastel acquiesced.

"What descriptor would you add to your name?" Pastel asked Sara.

Without hesitation, she replied, "Sara the Practical."

"Why practical?"

"For me, being practical has meant a willingness to set aside my aspirations for the greater good."

"I assume you mean your husband and children."

"And my mother. You may recall I characterized my life as a series of interruptions."

Pastel nodded.

"It seemed that every time I tried to connect with my love of art, something arose to steer me off course. When I graduated from college, for example, I won a fellowship to study art in Paris. Then David asked me to marry him. After I said yes, I discovered that fellows needed to be single. So, I started working on a Masters of Fine Art while David completed his dissertation at the University of Virginia. When he earned his doctorate, David landed an excellent position at Stanford. I was only part way through my Master's program. I decided to teach art at a private school in Palo Alto so we could afford to buy a house. I loved teaching art to bright and talented young people.

"I sense another interruption is coming," Pastel commented.

"Correct. I got pregnant and had to stop teaching. I planned to return to teaching after my maternity leave was up, but Randy had some health issues as a baby. David and I felt it was best for me to stay home."

"Did you eventually return to teaching when Randy and Marie

were older?

"That was my plan, but then my mother came to live with us after she was diagnosed with Alzheimer's disease. I cared for her for two years until she passed away."

"Listening to you makes me very sad," Pastel responded. "Sad for you and sad for me. It seems like having the desire to pursue a dream just isn't enough."

"Let's change the subject. What would you like to do after lunch?"

"I'd like to ditch Mehmet and go to an art museum," Pastel responded.

"I know you're suggesting that because of me, but I think going to an art museum would be wonderful. Let's tell Mehmet. I'm paying him, after all."

When they finished eating, the women found Mehmet outside and expressed their interest in visiting an art museum. Mehmet apologized and told them that several new art centers were scheduled to open in 2023 to celebrate the hundredth anniversary of the Turkish Republic, but at present Istanbul lacked any first-rate art centers.

Sara and Pastel were skeptical. Mehmet obviously intended to conduct his usual tour regardless of their interests. In order to return to the European side of the Bosphorus, Mehmet directed Sara and Pastel to a nearby dock where ferries were arriving and departing. They purchased tickets and rushed to catch a boat getting ready to leave.

Once on board, Mehmet suggested they roost in the dining area and enjoy a cup of tea. An empty table was located, and Mehmet sat across from Sara and Pastel. After gesturing to an attendant to bring tea, he asked if he could take a photograph of the two women for "publicity purposes." When Pastel questioned what he meant, Mehmet said that he liked to have a record of the people he has taken on tours.

"Do you enjoy being a tour guide?" Sara asked. "I would think it gets tiresome always visiting the same places."

"Ah! But the people are always different," he responded. "Some have even invited me to visit them."

"Have you ever considered going to places that your customers would like to see?" Pastel asked.

"That would require learning about all the places to see in Istanbul. Even I couldn't do that."

Sara asked Mehmet what he did before becoming a tour guide. He reported growing up in a poor region of eastern Turkey and dreaming of playing professional soccer. As a young man he excelled at the game and was invited to play for a major team in Istanbul. After eight years of "stardom", a hip injury ended Mehmet's career. He enrolled in a college program for tour guides and got married. When Pastel asked about children, he shook his head, then added, "My wife is young and fertile, so perhaps there is still hope." Pastel blushed. Mehmet excused himself and went out on deck for a cigarette.

"Is this just the way life is?" Pastel asked. "Everyone eventually has to abandon what they dreamed of doing." Sara did not respond.

Once the ferry docked, the threesome walked to a commercial area and visited a spice market, the mosque where Mehmet said he went to pray, and an enormous indoor bazaar packed with hundreds of stalls and small shops. Mehmet gave Sara and Pastel an hour to squeeze their way through crowds of shoppers and pleading shopkeepers. The bazaar was both dazzling and dizzying. After an hour, all Sara and Pastel wanted to do was locate Mehmet and return to their hotel.

Mehmet, however, had one more sight they needed to see, the light show at the Basillica Cistern. A three-block walk brought the party to a ticket booth. The subterranean cistern dated back to Roman times when it served as a water storage facility. Descending into semi-darkness, Sara and Pastel encountered dozens of stone columns supporting the cistern's ceiling.

When all the ticket holders had assembled, the lights were turned off. Total darkness produced gasps from the visitors. A few seconds later the light show commenced. Images representing different periods in Istanbul's history were projected onto the cistern walls while a narrator explained what was being shown.

When the light show ended, the crowd filed up the stairs and into the bright sunshine. It took a few moments for eyes to adjust. Sara and Pastel eventually spotted Mehmet with his arm around a young female tour guide. They told him the light show had been entertaining. He asked if they planned to purchase any souvenirs in Istanbul because he knew of some special stores off the beaten track. Sara said her experiences were the best souvenirs.

Mehmet looked puzzled. "What about for others? You have no

family back home?"

Sara did not answer, but Pastel told Mehmet that they made arrangements for dinner and needed to return to their hotel. The two women held hands as Mehmet guided them to the tram and informed them which stop was closest to the hotel and how much to pay for the ride. Sara offered Mehmet a tip, but he refused to accept it, claiming it was an honor to spend the day with such lovely ladies. Before leaving them, Mehmet gave Sara and Pastel his business card in case they ever returned.

While the two waited for the appropriate tram, Sara asked if Pastel had signed up for any excursions on the cruise. She said she had not had time to think about excursions, and asked Sara the same question.

"I only signed up for one tour. It goes from Kavala, our first port of call, to a place called Xanthi. It sounded exotic. Why don't you sign up, too. Maybe we'll have an adventure. Who knows?"

Pastel smiled. "An adventure definitely would be fun, but right now I'd settle for a life."

CHAPTER 4

Sara awoke and remembered her luggage needed to be in the hallway by eight thirty so it could be transferred to the Argonaut. The clock by her bed read seven fifty-three. She rose quickly, donned her robe, and chose an outfit for the day. After making certain everything meant to be packed had been, she rolled her suitcases into the hallway. Her time slot for registering to board the ship was between eleven and twelve that morning. No need to rush.

The morning was spent leisurely soaking in the bathtub, shaving her legs, getting dressed, and ordering room service. Sara was glad she no longer bothered with shoulder length hair and makeup. Just a little eye liner for definition. She was looking more like her hippie mother than she cared to admit. The only reason Sara had worn her hair longer was because David liked it that way. She needed half an hour to dry it and comb it out. The low maintenance look, as she called it, appealed to her practical nature.

By eleven o'clock, Sara was standing in line at Istanbul's enormous port facility waiting to register for the cruise. Check-in required a passport and proof of vaccination. After clearing registration, Sara proceeded up the gangplank and then took the ship's elevator to her penthouse cabin on the ninth deck. Her luggage was waiting for her.

After opening the curtains, checking out the veranda, and examining the well-appointed bathroom, Sara unpacked. The small framed photograph of David standing in front of Monticello was placed on the dressing table.

A bottle of champagne was chilling in an ice bucket beside the coffee table. Sara debated whether to uncork it now or wait until later. Seeing that the butler had left a stopper for the bottle, she went ahead and popped the cork, poured herself a flute of bubbly liquid, and toasted David. "Why aren't you here with me like you're supposed to be?" she quietly said.

With lots of time before the ship embarked, Sara decided to tour the Argonaut. She and David had taken several cruises on mega-ships to the Caribbean, but this was her first time on a vessel designed for less than a thousand passengers. She chose to begin her tour on the twelfth deck and work her way down the central staircase. The top deck housed a large lounge with a semi-circular bar, dozens of tables with upholstered chairs, and a sitting area for viewing the ship's progress. An attendant told Sara that high tea was scheduled every day at four in the lounge. The bar offered two-for-one drinks from five to six thirty. Sara visualized the lounge area full of people, most of whom were couples or part of large groups.

Descending to the eleventh deck, Sara found the writer-in-residence room, a room for cooking demonstrations and lessons, a library, two specialty restaurants, and a coffee bar. Stopping at the coffee bar, she ordered a latte, then noticed Pastel and her father sipping Americanos. Pastel invited her to join them.

Brendan Greene fit Sara's image of a writer. He wore wire-rim glasses and a scarf wrapped loosely around his neck. An unlit pipe hung out one side of his mouth. He made an effort to rise from his wheelchair to greet Sara, but she insisted he remain seated.

"Normally I would stand to greet a lovely lady," he mumbled, "but as you can see, I am far from normal."

"What would you normally do to greet a homely woman?" Sara inquired with a smile.

"Touche, Mrs. Castle. In the future, I must choose my words

more carefully. May I take this opportunity to express my appreciation for your kindness to my daughter. She enjoyed seeing Istanbul with you."

"The feeling is mutual. Pastel made a delightful companion. She helped keep our guide at bay."

"Men certainly create their share of problems, Mrs. Castle," Brendan replied as he picked up his coffee.

"That's a major theme in most of Dad's books," Pastel added. "What is it you say men need to be?" Pastel asked her father.

"Men need to be men is my mantra, but some men also need to be tenderized."

"Like cheap steak?" Sara asked.

"Precisely."

"Do you intend to go on any excursions?" Sara asked Brendan. He replied that most of his time would be taken up with his writer-in-residence duties, including several lectures and some classes on journaling and writing fiction. Getting around in a wheelchair in a foreign country, he added, usually is a nightmare.

"I've been ravaged by rheumatoid arthritis, Mrs. Castle. Can you believe that my body actually is attacking itself?"

"It's a shame your wife couldn't join you on the cruise," Sara commented.

"If she were here, I suspect she'd be attacking me as well. Perhaps Pastel did not inform you. My wife and I are socially distant at present."

Sara understood "socially distancing" to mean they were separated. "I apologize," she said. "These days it's a mistake to assume anything."

"Sage observation, Mrs. Castle."

"Please call me Sara."

"I shall be delighted to do so."

"Father has told me," Pastel announced, "that he does not require my assistance while on the ship. We have a butler assigned to us."

"He can keep me supplied with coffee, whiskey, and the occasional courtesan," Brendan added playfully.

"Father, you've only just met Sara. She's not accustomed to your wit."

"Ten thousand pardons, Sara. What I believe Pastel might have been getting at earlier is she hopes you might include her in some of your land-based activities. That is, assuming you're able to evade the company of some libidinous Lothario."

"Father!" Pastel exclaimed.

Sara laughed. "I thought we agreed that assumptions are unwise."

"Point made, ever so subtly, Sara." Brendan offered a benign smile.

While Pastel mentioned several places she wanted to explore during the cruise, Sara finished her latte. Then she excused herself to complete her tour of the Argonaut. As she left, she invited Pastel and Brendan to join her in the bar for two-for-one drinks that evening.

Brendan called out, "In case you run out of things to do, I'd be honored for you to attend one of my writing workshops."

Sara turned around. "I'm afraid words are not my forte, Brendan. I'm almost certain, in fact, that I no longer have a forte."

Making her way down to the tenth deck, Sara found a health spa, outdoor swimming pool, snack bar, large dining room for cafeteria-style meals, and several activity rooms. Decks nine to seven were devoted to passenger cabins, while deck six contained several offices along with more cabins. The last deck open to passengers was deck five. It contained a large room with theater-style seating, several shops, a grand dining room, two specialty restaurants, a casino, the registration center, and various headquarters for passenger services. During her tour Sara encountered lots of arriving adults, but no children. She wondered if David purposely chose a cruise line that did not cater to families.

At four thirty, passengers were instructed over the ship's intercom to bring their life jackets to the assembly area posted on their cabin doors. Sara found her life jacket in the closet and proceeded to a sitting area opposite the casino, her designated assembly point. Instructions were given about how to put on the life jacket and what to do in the event of an emergency. As she listened, Sara couldn't help envisioning a chaotic scene in which passengers needed to evacuate the ship. The mass confusion of a Hieronymus Bosch painting popped into her head, though she was not troubled by the image.

Once the safety instructions had been completed, the captain announced that the Argonaut was ready to depart from Istanbul. Passengers rushed outside to observe the departure. Less interested in seeing the Argonaut leave port than in taking advantage of two-for-one drinks, Sara walked up seven flights of stairs to the lounge bar.

When she entered the bar area, Sara discovered another woman who apparently had the same idea. She was chatting with the burly, white-jacketed bartender. The woman appeared to be very slender, almost frail, with skin the color of coffee with cream. She wore black pants and a black, long-sleeved blouse. Sara guessed the woman was in her late sixties and not in good health.

The woman gestured for Sara to join her. As she took a seat, Sara was struck by the woman's eyes. They conveyed an intensity, even defiance, that belied her frailty. Sara got the impression this was no ordinary woman.

"I thought I'd be the first person to take advantage of two-for-one drinks," Sara announced cheerfully.

"Welcome to my office," the woman replied. "You're not even the second person to arrive."

Sara looked around, but didn't see any other customers. She gave the woman a puzzled look, then asked, "I didn't count the bartender, did I?"

In a thick Eastern European accent, the bartender interjected, "Very bad mistake. Must always count the bartender."

All three laughed. The woman introduced herself as Simone

Baker from St. Louis. She asked if Sara was traveling alone. Sara explained that she had planned to cruise with her husband, but he was killed in a terrible automobile accident just before the Pandemic struck.

"Well, at least you didn't have to watch your husband become enslaved to drugs. That can be worse than death."

Sara couldn't help wondering what life experience prompted Simone's unusual comment, but she didn't feel like questioning her about it. Her mood was upbeat, and she intended for it to stay that way.

Overhearing what the two women had said, the bartender said he was sorry to hear of such sadness. "Please call me Gyorgy," he announced. "I must be husband for all women traveling alone on the Argonaut."

"Sounds like you're going to be busy tonight," Sara laughed. She pulled out a pen and notepad from her purse. "How do you spell your name?" David always made a point of remembering the names of bartenders and servers.

"G-Y-O-R-G-Y."

"Sounds like Guy Orgy to me," Simone chuckled.

"No time for orgy. Must mix drinks. What I get for you?" he asked.

The Argonaut began to vibrate as it pulled away from the dock. Simone ordered a bourbon Manhattan straight up. Sara requested French chardonnay.

Sara told Simone that she was born in northern California, but lived much of her adult life in Charlottesville, Virginia. She and her husband were students at the University of Virginia. They moved away for a while, but eventually returned when David was hired by the university's development office.

Simone indicated that she had several colleagues at the University of Virginia, and she praised the university's efforts to acknowledge the role of enslaved workers in building and maintaining Jefferson's masterpiece. Simone was in the process of explaining that she recently retired from a professorship at Washington University when Pastel walked in.

Sara introduced Pastel to Simone and Gyorgy and invited her to join them. The young woman took a seat and ordered a Cosmopolitan, which prompted Sara to accuse her of watching too many re-runs of "Sex and the City."

Now that the ship was sailing, the bar began to fill up. Two additional bartenders joined Gyorgy. A white-haired man with a gold chain around his neck and a tan as dark as Simone's skin sat down next to Simone. Sara guessed he'd already had a few drinks. The man introduced himself as Wade Wilson from Waco, Texas, and, without being asked, said he was a widower on his ninth cruise. Simone reached out, tapped the man's hand, and started speaking rapidly in French. Sara and Pastel could hardly contain themselves as the man stood up and walked away.

Continuing to share her background, Simone said she held the McCoy Chair in Literature and Culture until her retirement. She went on to explain that she became fluent in French in order to study black writers who went to Paris during the twenties and thirties. Then she offered a suggestion.

"When I started a new semester, I used to break the ice by asking students to reveal something about themselves that most people didn't know. I'd kick things off by saying that when I was their age, I was a blues singer. They were always surprised. Then I'd add with mock seriousness that if they failed to complete assignments on time, they, too, would be singing the blues."

"Very clever," Pastel observed. "I'm one of those students who struggled to finish assignments on time. My father accused me of being a perfectionist. I kept revising my papers until the very last minute."

"At least you can write," Sara replied. "I preferred to paint pictures. That was fine for my art classes, but it didn't go over well in English literature and calculus."

"So, you're an artist?" Simone inquired.

"Only in my dreams these days."

"That's a good place to start," Simone said in a serious tone.

"And how about you, young lady? Are you gainfully employed when you're not cruising the Mediterranean?"

Pastel took a sip of her Cosmopolitan, trying not to spill the full-to-the-rim drink. "I was trained to be a social worker. After I completed my Master's degree, I worked in a women's shelter in upstate New York."

"Sounds like very challenging work," Simone noted.

"Too challenging, I'm afraid. Being around women, many of them my age or younger, who had experienced traumatic events in their lives gave me the dismals."

"The dismals?" Sara asked.

"That was our code word for depression at the shelter. I began having nightmares that one day I'd wind up a resident in a shelter. The work was terribly frustrating. We'd think a woman finally had turned her life around. She'd check herself out of the shelter and go right back to the abusive bastard who screwed up her life in the first place."

"I take it you quit," Simone said.

"I did," Pastel responded with a grimace. "My father is a writer and needed someone to word process his work. He still uses a type-writer. Publishers these days don't accept typewritten manuscripts."

"Might I have heard of your father," Simone asked.

"Brendan Greene. He's quite well known."

"Well known, yes. Well-liked, that depends."

Gyorgy brought Pastel her second Cosmopolitan and Sara another glass of chardonnay. Then he stared at Simone's half-full glass. "You no like Gyorgy's Manhattan?"

"Your Manhattan is delightful. I prefer to nurse my drink."

"Passengers get two for one until six thirty."

"One will be plenty, Gyorgy. I'm on medication."

"Manhattan is better medicine," Gyorgy replied as he left to wait on another customer.

Sara couldn't help reflecting on what Pastel said about working in a women's shelter. She pictured a group of old-before-their-time women sitting around a room full of discarded furniture watching soap operas on a secondhand television. Everything was beige, including the residents. The notion suddenly struck Sara that Pastel actually might have been a resident, not a social worker. She recalled how uncomfortable Pastel felt around Mehmet. So far Pastel had mentioned no men in her life other than her father. Of course, Sara reasoned, Pastel also could be gay or asexual.

"I told you something others don't know about me," Simone pointed out. "What about you, Pastel?"

Pastel thought for a moment. "How's this? I don't particularly care for my father's novels, especially those that focus on what he calls the crisis of manhood and the feminized male."

"I'm glad to hear you say that," Sara chimed in. "I only read his Oh! Men, but I didn't care for it. Too one-sided."

Simone took a tiny sip of her Manhattan. "I am in full agreement. I know your father's work, Pastel. He writes as if the only issues that matter are ones important to well-to-do white men. He ignores black men and expresses hostility toward gay men. Nonetheless, I'll say this about his work. The matter of what it means to be a man in today's world is an important one and worthy of addressing."

"So, how about your little-known fact?" Pastel asked Sara.

Sara turned to face Simone. Earlier I mentioned to Pastel that I took care of my mother for two years after she was diagnosed with Alzheimer's disease. What I didn't say is that I have become fearful I could inherit the disease. Mom's mother also had Alzheimer's. The prospect of losing all my memories is frightening. Sara fell silent.

Simone did not respond, apparently lost in her own thoughts.

Pastel finally spoke up, asking Simone if she planned to go on an excursion when they reached Kavala. Simone shook her head. Sara asked if she'd like to visit Xanthi with Pastel and her.

"You do know that trouble travels in threes, don't you," Simone responded with a weary smile. "I appreciate the invitation. Let me think about it. Now I must return to my room."

When Simone stood up, Sara realized how truly slight she was, like a Giacometti sculpture. She wanted to ask Simone if she needed assistance getting back to her room, but her intuition told her to hold off.

Pastel was the next to leave, saying she promised to take her father to the ship's seafood restaurant. "If I don't insist that he goes out to eat, he'll just remain in the room and order whiskey and something unhealthy to nibble on."

Sara suggested that Pastel meet her tomorrow in the sitting area on deck five. An announcement would be made when passengers were able to disembark. After finishing her drink and leaving a generous tip for Gyorgy, she went to the buffet dining room for dinner. Later she strolled around the ship for a while admiring its extensive art collection and thinking about Simone. There was a story there, to be sure. How does a woman go from being a blues singer to a professor?

Back in her room, Sara undressed, picked up Nikos Kazantzakis's Zorba the Greek, the book she chose to bring on the cruise, and read until her eyes began to close. She removed her short nightgown and stretched out on the king-sized bed that had been intended for two. The smooth cotton sheets felt cool and luxurious. Sara began to move her hands lightly over her breasts, then slowly down her torso and between her thighs the way David used to do. Closing her eyes, she pictured him leaning on his elbow next to her and growing increasingly excited as she became aroused.

CHAPTER 5

THURSDAY, SEPTEMBER 15, 2022

The alarm clock buzzed at six, interrupting an erotic dream in which Sara was an observer rather than a participant. Suddenly she remembered why she set the alarm for such an early hour. After missing her regular workouts for almost a week, she needed to stretch and lift and jog. Fifty-five-year-old bodies did not stay fit and functional without some coaxing. The Argonaut's state-of-the-art fitness center with its line-up of exercise machines and buff instructors beckoned.

When she arrived at the fitness center, Sara discovered that other passengers had similar ideas. Only one elliptical machine was unused, so she mounted it and began her workout. Instead of watching the attached video screen, she gazed out the large window as the Argonaut approached the port of Kavala on the northeast coast of Greece. In the distance she noticed hillsides full of white houses with red tile roofs. A rocky promontory jutted out into the harbor and appeared to be topped by a fortress. She regretted not bringing her camera to the fitness center.

When her workout was over, Sara showered and dressed, then made her way to the buffet breakfast. While the bar the previous evening had been packed with couples by the time Sara left, the dining room this morning was populated mostly by unaccompanied individuals. Sara surmised that some spouses preferred to sleep late. On vacation, David typically was the late riser. Sara considered sitting with someone, but she didn't feel like making what David referred to as small talk, at least not until she'd had two cups of coffee.

Collecting a bowl of fresh fruit, a croissant, and an omelet with Swiss cheese, Sara carefully navigated the archipelago of tables on her way to an empty table by a window. The ship had begun to rock a bit as it maneuvered toward the pier, so keeping her balance with both hands holding dishes was challenging. No sooner was Sara safely seated than a server magically appeared with coffee.

As Sara ate, she thought about the upcoming excursion to Xanthi. What she desired was a genuine adventure, something out of the ordinary. Months of COVID cautions had left her craving new experiences. She loved Bertrand Piccard's well-known quote: "Routine is more dangerous than adventure." Boredom with life, she understood, could be lethal.

If one word characterized her life since the Pandemic's onset, it was routine. Rise at six. Egg on toast every other day. Cereal otherwise. Workout from eight to nine thirty. Watch Marcus on Tuesdays and Thursdays. Grocery shopping Wednesday. Laundry Friday. Glass of wine at four while watching CNN. Coffee with Marie on Saturday. Netflix from seven to nine, then bed.

Sara tried to recall the last time she experienced some semblance of an adventure, anything unexpected or amazing. Was her honeymoon the last time? Could three decades have passed without a real heart-pounding, eye-popping adventure, not just some vicarious thrill on television or an activity where she was a spectator instead of a participant? She cautioned herself not to exaggerate. There must have been adventures along the way, but David always planned their trips so carefully that unexpected happenings were uncommon. Sara finally decided to blame her declining memory for not recalling at least a few adventures.

As for routines, Sara had to admit that her daily rituals enabled her to survive the shock of David's death and the fears created by the COVID crisis. Without them, just getting up in the morning would have been difficult. Lately, though, Sara felt her routines were sapping the life out of her. Dwelling on her routine life and lack of adventure was generating a dark mood for Sara. Fortunately, Pastel showed up just in time to prevent a full-scale funk.

"Are you ready to explore the wonders of Xanthi?" Pastel enthused as she approached.

"I've never been a reader. Give me five minutes to retrieve a light sweater, just in case the bus is air conditioned. I'll meet you in the departure lounge."

"It's supposed to hit ninety degrees today," Pastel announced after quickly checking the weather app on her cell phone. "Let's hope the bus is air conditioned."

Five minutes later Sara and Pastel met in the crowded lounge on deck five where everyone with morning excursions awaited permission to disembark. Simone was not there.

Soon thereafter the cruise director announced it was time for all passengers bound for Xanthi to depart. Still no Simone. Pastel offered to phone Simone, but she didn't know her cell phone or cabin number. The two surmised Simone was not feeling well and decided to remain on the ship. Just as they approached the gangplank, Simone arrived looking haggard. Sara asked if she had become seasick during the night. Simone apologized for being late and attributed her tardiness to having drunk too much at the bar last evening. Sara and Pastel just looked at each other, but didn't say anything. They both knew Simone only finished half of her Manhattan.

The trio was registered for bus number seven, which they spotted several hundred yards from the pier in a lot with a dozen other buses. Simone expressed what Sara was thinking. "I hope all those buses aren't headed for Xanthi."

When they reached bus seven, their tour guide took each person's ticket, and they boarded the bus. All the seats near the front already were occupied, so they moved to seats near the rear door. Pastel and Simone sat together on one side of the aisle, while Sara sat across from them and next to their handbags. While they waited for the bus to fill, Pastel asked Simone why she decided to retire.

"I could see the handwriting on the wall. No one is interested in an English literature major anymore. They want business, medicine, law, or engineering. Some colleges have actually eliminated their graduate program in English."

"That's terrible. When I went to Yale, it was because of its wonderful English department. I wanted to major in English and become a writer, but Dad talked me out of it. I wound up in sociology along with half the football team.

"Being a writer was once a respectable profession," Simone asserted. "So many of us have been influenced by great writers. Today, though, true literature is rare. Writing has become a business like everything else. It's controlled by large publishers and guided by social media and algorithms. If they read at all, people only want to read material that confirms their biases. An open mind these days is as rare as a politician with integrity."

Hearing Simone's remarks, Sara asked, "What area of literature did you specialize in?"

"I became fascinated with the intersection of literature and culture, how literature helps to shape culture and vice versa. That interest led me to investigate why many black writers and artists migrated to France after the First World War."

Before she could elaborate, the tour guide picked up her microphone and asked if any passengers had visited Greece before. Simone raised her hand along with almost half the other passengers. Next, she asked if anyone had seen Xanthi. No one raised their hand.

As the bus sped out of Kavala and onto a modern highway, the guide, an attractive middle-aged woman who said her name was Athena and joked that some people thought she was a goddess, offered background information about their destination. Xanthi had been a colony of the Ottoman Empire until the Bulgarian army captured the city during the First World War. After Bulgaria and its allies lost the war, the Greek army took command of Xanthi. It became known as a thriving center of the tobacco trade. The city's many brightly painted mansions are evidence of its prosperous past. Greeks refer to Xanthi as the city of a thousand colors.

Sara glanced at Simone during the guide's comments and noticed that her eyes were closed. Clearly, she wasn't feeling well. Sara hoped it wasn't the COVID virus.

Eventually the bus reached Xanthi and parked beside a large plaza with a bell tower topped by a blue and white Greek flag. People milled about among vendors selling coffee, pastries, clothing, souvenirs, and fresh produce. Café tables with umbrellas ringed the plaza. Before leaving the bus, Athena instructed her group to spend half an hour exploring the area before gathering at the base of the bell tower for a guided tour. Given the heat, she advised everyone to stay hydrated. Pastel gently nudged Simone to awaken her and shared what the guide had said.

The three women agreed that the first order of business was purchasing something cool to drink and locating a table in the shade. Heat radiated off the plaza's concrete surface. Sara had doubts about Simone's ability to undertake a walking tour. While Pastel and Simone bought bottled water, Sara found a vendor selling caps and purchased three.

Passengers from bus seven eventually re-assembled at the bell tower as instructed. Most complained about the intense heat and their failure to bring appropriate clothing. Athena apologized and promised to find shade whenever the group stopped for a mini-lecture.

The group meandered through several affluent residential neighborhoods consisting of large, but not particularly attractive mansions. Based on what she was seeing, Sara felt the city of a thousand colors was actually very drab. It didn't take long for her to tire of hearing about which tobacco baron lived in which mansion. Simone was struggling to keep up with the group. When the tour guide stopped to give everyone a chance to rest, Sara asked Simone and Pastel if they minded quitting the tour and returning to the plaza to sit in the shade. Both women readily agreed.

As they backtracked to the plaza, Sara commented, "If this is what the excursions are going to be like, I'm glad we only signed up for one. My idea of adventure is not walking around in stifling heat listening to boring local history. David would have hated it."

"I guess it's just as well that I couldn't hear what Athena was saying," Simone added.

When they reached the plaza, Pastel found an unoccupied table with an umbrella. Sara went to a vendor, purchased bottled water, and returned to her two companions.

After scanning the people gathered on the plaza, Simone announced, "I feel like a penguin in Polynesia. I don't see a single black person."

Sara and Pastel confirmed her observation after studying the crowd. Pastel brought up Simone's interest in black emigres to

France.

"When I was in college," she replied, "I undertook a study abroad program in France and met James Baldwin. It was the seventies, and he lived in Saint-Paul-de-Vence. Blacks back home were criticizing him for losing touch with what it meant to be black in the United States. He told me that blacks who fought in France during the First World War found the French were more accepting of them than American whites. That got me thinking about French culture and what made it less racist than American culture."

Sara noted that she had watched a fascinating documentary about Josephine Baker and how the French loved her.

Simone smiled. "You know my last name is Baker, and I'm from St. Louis, just like Josephine. I always wondered if we were related. Wouldn't that have been something?"

Pastel whispered that a woman had been staring at them since they sat down. Sara looked over Simone's shoulder and saw a short woman wearing a tattered abaya and a hijab. She looked weary and limped as she approached the group. One leg appeared to be shorter than the other.

"I think we are about to be visited by a beggar," Pastel said.

"A thousand pardons, madams. Could you spare a few euros so I can buy food?"

Sara was surprised the woman spoke English so clearly. "You speak English very well. Would you like some water?" Sara offered her an unopened bottle.

"You are very kind. I have not eaten in two days."

Pastel brought a chair from another table so the woman could sit down.

"I am a refugee from Syria."

"Where did you learn English?" Simone inquired.

"I was a teacher in Syria. I studied English in school."

"Do you have family in Syria?" Sara asked.

"My husband was killed. We lived in Aleppo. I do not know if my parents survived the bombing."

Simone shook her head. "Never have so many lived in comfort while so many struggled to survive. What a world we have."

"Have the Greeks been able to help you?" Pastel asked.

The woman, whose name was Latifa, explained that she was sent to a refugee camp when she crossed the border from Turkey, but conditions in the camp were terrible. Women refugees were frequently raped and beaten. She was advised to find her way to Spain or Germany, where refugees were treated better, but she spoke neither Spanish or German.

Sara explained that the three of them were on a cruise and would be departing soon to return to their ship. Then she reached into her fanny pack and took out a hundred-euro bill. "I wish I could do more for you, Latifa." Pastel and Simone also gave her money.

"Allah be praised," Latifa cried gratefully.

"What will you do now?" Pastel asked.

"What can I do? I live without a future. But it is good there are kind people in the world, not just murderers of the innocent."

Latifa limped off. The women sat for a while, saying nothing. A wave of anguish swept over Sara. She desperately had wanted to offer Latifa a practical way to deal with her misfortune, but nothing came to mind. It grieved Sara to feel helpless. Latifa's comment that she lived without a future haunted her. Sara wondered if it applied to her as well.

Pastel spotted the tour guide and her flock at the far end of the plaza. They looked exhausted and unhappy. Bus number seven pulled up at just about the same time. The three women were overjoyed to sink into their seats and enjoy the air conditioning. Grumbling from other passengers could be heard as they boarded the bus. Apparently, Sara, Pastel, and Simone weren't the only ones disappointed with Xanthi and deflated by the intense heat. Sara felt sorry for Athena, who had no control over the weather or the itinerary.

Sara asked Simone if she was having second thoughts about coming on the cruise.

"I admit regretting our visit to Xanthi, and I did have second thoughts about going on the cruise. Then I asked myself, what have I got to lose? I'm retired. I have no family. I sold my home. So big deal, I'm not feeling well. I could not feel well in St. Louis or on the ship."

"I admire your spunk," Sara responded.

"Spunk, perhaps, or more likely ennui."

"Well, I have an idea, ladies, and I guarantee it'll be better than my choice of today's excursion," Sara announced. "Can we meet on deck twelve bar at five thirty this evening?"

Simone agreed and closed her eyes. Pastel agreed and pulled out a notebook and a pen from her backpack. Sara leaned back and thought about Latifa. She tried to visualize the poor woman's trek from Syria to Turkey and on to Greece. Nothing in her own experience, however, enabled her to picture what such a journey must have been like. Ever since David died, Sara had felt sorry for herself. Now those feelings prompted guilt. After all, she still had her children and grandchild, her health, the resources to live comfortably, and thirty years' worth of memories with David.

Sara and Pastel walked up to the bar on deck twelve at the same time. They greeted Gyorgy, and he asked about their excursion. When both women responded by frowning, he promised to be extra generous with their drinks. A little later Simone arrived looking rested and revived.

"So, Sara, what's your big idea?" Simone asked. "Have you retained male escorts for us?"

"Only one," Sara replied with a wink. "I've hired a driver to take us to Meteora tomorrow after we dock at Volos. No big bus. No being herded around. Just the three of us and Mikail."

"What's in Meteora?" Pastel asked.

"Lots of monasteries perched precariously on enormous rocks. The pictures I've seen are incredible. Scenes in a James Bond movie actually were filmed there."

Simone and Pastel agreed that Sara's plan sounded a lot better than going on another cruise-sponsored excursion. Gyorgy overheard Sara's proposal and offered a toast to "a day with the monks."

"And nuns," Sara added. "There's also a convent, I understand."

Pastel turned to Gyorgy and said, "If you don't see me here tomorrow evening, it's because I entered the convent."

"Too young for a convent," he responded. "Need to find a good man." Gyorgy departed to wait on other customers.

"Why is it that people think a woman needs a man?" Pastel asked no one in particular. She quickly turned to Sara. "I'm so sorry. Please forgive my insensitivity."

"Sounds like you haven't had good experiences with men," Simone observed.

"Did I offend you as well?"

"Not at all, my dear. I learned long ago that the only person I can count on is myself."

"Were you ever married?" Sara asked.

Simone paused to sip her Manhattan. "It wasn't much of a marriage, at least by your standards. I was seventeen, just out of high school and singing in a blues band. He was the lead guitarist. We had a fling and decided to get married. He was pretty heavily into drugs, but I thought I could help him. I was mistaken. When he got high, he became abusive. The abuse got worse when he learned that a record company executive wanted me to audition without the rest of the band."

"Did you leave him?" Pastel asked.

"Actually, he left me. I missed my period and was certain I was pregnant. When I told him, he disappeared. As it turned out, I wasn't pregnant, but thinking I was saved me from making a huge mistake."

Gyorgy informed the group that the ship's jazz ensemble was getting ready to perform. "They make wonderful music. Very talented. Very loud. All from Ukraine."

Conversation at the bar was impossible due to its proximity to the stage. Sara and Pastel collected their second drink and moved with Simone to a remote table. Once again, Simone left her Manhattan half-finished. Sara explained that her friends needed to meet in the departure lounge at nine the next morning. Pastel finished her drink and excused herself so she could join her father for dinner.

Sara caught Simone staring at the jazz ensemble and tapping her fingers to the beat of the music. Several numbers later they played "Someone to Watch over Me." Simone closed her eyes. "That's one of my favorite songs," she exclaimed.

"How'd you become a blues singer?" Sara asked. "I always pictured blues vocalists as mature women with worldly wrinkles and ample breasts."

"Some folks are just born with the blues. Call it fate. The blues is part of their DNA. I never knew my father. My mother ran off with a Jamaican drug dealer when I was eight years old. If my aunt Pearl hadn't taken me in, I don't know where I would have wound up."

Sara began to cry. Simone and her story of overcoming obstacles triggered admiration, and for reasons Sara couldn't explain, admiration invariably led to tears. Despite Simone's health issues, there was an aura about the woman, a sturdiness that conveyed a powerful will to survive and an insistence on living on her own terms. Sara would have loved to paint Simone, that is if she still was a practicing artist. Capturing the quiet defiance in her friend's eyes would have been a worthy challenge.

When the ensemble took a break, Simone told Sara she wished there was some way they could help Pastel. "The poor girl seems completely adrift. I don't know what happened to her, but she's got scars."

"One thing's for certain," Sara declared. "Pastel needs a future, just like Latifa. When she talks, she never mentions looking forward to anything."

CHAPTER 6

FRIDAY, SEPTEMBER 16, 2022

Sara and Simone sensed something was wrong when Pastel arrived at the departure lounge on Friday morning. Instead of briskly approaching, she moved haltingly, taking a few steps, then stopping, then taking a few more steps. The young woman's usual smile and engaging persona were absent, replaced by a flat affect and frown.

"Are you all right?" Simone asked.

"Not really," was her terse reply.

As the three companions awaited the announcement to disembark, Pastel shared the reason for her troubled appearance. It seemed she and her father got into an argument at dinner the previous evening. He told her she needed to get on with her life and urged her to develop a career plan. When he asked what she would do if he suddenly died, she responded that she might die before him. He got very upset and insisted he would not allow her to waste her life word processing his work.

"I went to bed last night feeling like an utter failure," Pastel sobbed. "I know Dad's right and only wants what's best for me, but my lack of direction is largely his fault. I wanted to pursue a career as a writer until he talked me out of it."

"That was wrong of him," Simone declared. "If becoming a

writer is your dream, you must pursue it."

Sara listened with interest, but refrained from saying anything. She, after all, had abandoned her dream of becoming an artist. What advice could she offer Pastel? Do the practical thing and find a job so you can support yourself? Find a husband who'll take care of you? Pastel's concerns struck too close to home, making Sara feel very uncomfortable.

The cruise director finally announced that passengers were free to leave the ship. Sara asked her friends to be on the lookout for a man holding a placard with his name, Mikail, on it. Pastel spotted him once they descended the gangplank and headed toward the exit gate. From a distance, she noted, he bore a striking resemblance to George Clooney. "If only," Sara replied.

"Yahsoo! Welcome to Volos," Mikail called out as the women approached. "I am honored to be your driver to Meteora. It is truly a remarkable place."

The women introduced themselves and followed Mikail to a small Mercedes bus. He asked when the Argonaut was scheduled to leave port, and Sara said seven o'clock. Mikail expressed relief that they would not have to rush. The journey, he said, would take around two hours, and he promised to share some information about Meteora when they got closer to their destination.

There was little conversation during the first part of the trip. Simone napped while Pastel stared at the passing countryside. Sara meanwhile wondered how Marcus was enjoying preschool in Charlottesville and if his mother had planned to enroll him in a similar program when they moved to Charlotte. She jotted a note to remind herself to send Marcus a postcard when the ship reached Santorini.

Mikail periodically fielded a question. "Do you like Greek food? Have you ever seen 'Zorba the Greek?' Do you think Biden will run for President again?" Sara usually responded to the group. She asked Mikail if he thought Greece and Turkey would go to war over disputed territory. He doubted it because each country's economy was in such bad shape.

After an hour, Simone opened her eyes and asked if they were close to Meteora. Mikail wondered if she required a restroom, and all three women responded that a restroom would be much appreciated. Soon thereafter he pulled off the highway into a commercial area with a petrol station and a café. The town of Larissa could be seen in the distance.

After going to the restroom and purchasing coffee and pastries, the journey continued. Simone asked Pastel if she had made up her mind regarding her father's advice to develop a career plan.

"I'm trained to be a social worker," she responded, but I'm not suited to handling other people's problems. I can't even help myself. Did you experience difficulty determining what you wanted to do in life?"

Simone considered Pastel's question. "Let me put it this way," she finally replied, "I knew what I didn't want to do before I knew what I wanted to do. I had learned that the life of a blues singer was usually an unhappy one. I didn't want to marry another loser or have children. Aunt Pearl encouraged me to apply to college. I qualified for a scholarship to attend Washington University because I had done well in high school. It was there that I discovered the life of a professor was a pretty good one. There were many opportunities to meet interesting people and travel plus I could live on my own terms as long as I was academically productive."

Sara listened with interest to Simone's response and wondered what her own life might have been like if she had finished an advanced degree and become a professor of art or art history. She spent a few minutes trying to visualize it, but failed to develop a clear picture. Sara took this to mean she wasn't cut out for academic life.

Soon Mikail indicated that they were getting close to Meteora. It was time for him to offer some background information on their destination. The name, Meteora, referred to a collection of huge rock columns on which rested a number of monasteries. Only the monastic complex at Mount Athos was larger. The oldest monastery at Meteora dates back to the fourteenth century.

"When you see these holy places," Mikail continued, "you will wonder how small groups of monks were able to reach the tops of these rock columns and construct churches and living quarters. I personally believe it was easier to build the Pyramids of Egypt." As Mikail continued with his travelog, he kept turning toward his three passengers. Sara did not intend for her second honeymoon to end in a traffic accident, so she insisted Mikail focus on the road ahead.

A few moments later Mikail suddenly veered off the main highway onto a secondary road. After passing a small, tourist-oriented settlement, the rock columns of Meteora came into view. It was hard to spot the monasteries perched on top. Once Mikail negotiated a series of switchbacks and steep inclines that had the riders complaining of queasy stomachs, the monasteries began to come into view. Sara thought they resembled fairy castles in the clouds.

Mikail pulled over at an observation point and pointed to one monastery dangling precariously on the edge of an enormous rock column. "Did anyone see the James Bond movie, 'For Your Eyes Only'?" he asked. Sara replied that she saw it because her husband was enthralled with Bond films. Mikail explained that the thrilling conclusion of the movie was filmed at the Monastery of the Holy Trinity. He suggested that anyone wanting photographs should shoot them where they were stopped because many of the monasteries were visible here.

Pastel grabbed her cell phone, Sara picked up her camera, and the three women stepped out of the bus. Sara held Simone's hand because the pavement was uneven. Pastel took a picture of Sara and Simone standing by a low rock wall separating observers from the abyss beyond. Simone admitted being fearful of heights and quickly moved away from the wall as soon as the picture was taken.

Sara snapped a few photos to show Marcus, then put her camera away. Mikail asked why she didn't take more pictures, and she told him the story of losing all of her carefully compiled photo albums in an attic fire. In a matter of minutes, the visual records of years of cherished experiences went up in flames.

"That's when I realized," Sara explained, "that taking photographs gave me permission to forget about what I was actually seeing. My goal was to possess pictures, not preserve memories."

Mikail looked perplexed by Sara's comments. Changing the subject, he pointed out that some of Meteora's monasteries had closed because fewer men were choosing the monastic life. Some of the remaining ones were not open to the public. He mentioned several that allowed tourists to visit. Pastel asked about convents, and Mikail answered there was only one, Agios Stefanos. Convents, he added, were also referred to as monasteries in the Greek Orthodox religion. Until 1961, Agios Stefanos housed monks. From the monastery the view of the plain stretching toward Kalabaka, in Mikail's judgment, was magnificent.

The three women discussed their options and agreed to visit Agios Stefanos. A brief drive brought them to a small parking area from which rose a lengthy flight of stone stairs. Mikail handed each woman bottled water and advised them to take the stairs slowly because of the heat. He also warned that the nuns might require them to cover their heads and legs before they entered the sanctuary. Scarfs and robes were available for those needing them. Mikail promised to be waiting in the parking lot when the group completed their visit.

"No beer while you wait for us," Simone instructed Mikail as the women headed off.

"No worries," he replied. "I prefer ouzo."

Gazing up at the steep stairs leading to Agios Stefanos, Simone quipped, "This must be how the nuns get to heaven."

Sara offered her hand to Simone, since sections of the stairway lacked railings. With periodic pauses to rest and drink water, the threesome took fifteen minutes to reach the top. They found themselves in a large courtyard filled with flowers and trees and surrounded on three sides by stone buildings with red tile roofs. Several clusters of visitors milled about the courtyard taking pictures and inspecting the gardens.

A large nun in a black habit and wearing around her neck a chain from which hung a wooden cross approached the three women and introduced herself as Sister Sophia. She explained that the original monastery was thought to have been built in the thirteen hundreds, but the current facility was constructed in 1798. By Meteora standards, it was recent. The nun offered to conduct a tour because she spoke English.

Simone expressed relief when they entered the church, which was much cooler than the courtyard. As the tour wound its way through various rooms dedicated to different purposes, Sara admired the frescoes depicting religious figures in colorful robes. Golden orbs framed their heads. Most figures looked straight ahead, as if they were examining onlookers. Sister Sophia noted that many of the frescoes and paintings were made by the residents of Agios Stefanos. While religious art was not Sara's favorite genre, she appreciated the ingenuity and effort required to create what she was viewing.

Twenty minutes into the tour, Pastel asked if a bathroom was nearby. Sister Sophia said toilet facilities for guests were off of the courtyard and down a flight of steps. Sara wondered if Pastel was unwell, since she had said very little on the bus and during the tour.

Pastel departed, and Sister Sophia resumed the tour, visiting workrooms where her colleagues undertook embroidery, painting, incense-making, and needlework. Simone asked how many nuns lived at the monastery, and Sister Sophia responded there were less than thirty.

"We try to be as self-sufficient as possible," she added. "Our order embraces discipline, dedication, and humility. This is not a life for everyone."

Sara was curious about the reason Sister Sophia became a nun, but she felt it was too personal a question to ask. Still, she couldn't help wondering whether some women sought the community of other women because they had bad experiences with men.

According to Sister Sophia, the Nazis believed that Greek monasteries harbored resistance fighters and refugees during the Second World War. As a result, Meteora was bombed and the monasteries were searched and looted.

"Pastel must have gotten lost," Simone exclaimed. "Shouldn't she have returned by now?"

"I speak from experience," Sister Sophia began. "It is very easy to get lost here. When I was a novice, I was always losing my way. I was told that all must lose their way before they find their way." She smiled and excused herself in order to conduct another tour.

"Hopefully she's not sick," Sara said. "I'd better check the restroom. Simone, why don't you have a seat in the church. If Pastel goes there before I return, just remain in the church."

Sara had no difficulty locating the restroom, but Pastel was not there. As she was leaving, a young woman arrived. Sara described Pastel and asked if the woman had seen her, but she spoke no English. The route to the restroom was not confusing. Sara found it hard to believe that a bright person like Pastel could have gotten lost.

When she returned to the courtyard, Sara asked an older woman who looked American if she had seen an attractive, dark-haired young woman recently. The woman said she saw someone who fit that description about twenty minutes earlier. She was perched on a low wall that jutted out from the rock column and appeared to be taking a selfie. The older woman warned her to be careful. If she slipped, her life would be over.

Sara was now concerned. She hurried to backtrack the route taken by Sister Sophia. The possibility that Pastel might have slipped and fallen to her death was too terrible to consider. Of course, there was also the other possibility, that Pastel fell on purpose. She clearly felt distraught after arguing with her father last night. Hadn't she admitted lacking a purpose in life? The more Sara considered the possibility of suicide, the more anxious and guilty she felt. It was her idea, after all, to visit Meteora, just as it had been her stupid pickleball accident that prevented her from accompanying David on his fateful business trip.

On the verge of panic, Sara tried to locate Sister Sophia. As she passed the kitchen where nuns prepared their meals, Sara thought she heard Pastel's voice. When she entered the dark room, Pastel was talking quietly to a young nun. The nun's face, the only visible part of her body, struck Sara as angelic with its rosy cheeks, gentle smile, and caring expression.

"Thank God," Sara exclaimed as she rushed to hug Pastel.

"We do a lot of thanking God here," the young nun replied.

"I'm so sorry," Pastel apologized. "I got lost trying to catch up with the tour. That's when I ran into Sister Thea. She speaks English, so I asked her about why women choose to enter a monastery. Can you believe she's from Chicago?"

After Sister Thea excused herself, Sara asked about the nun's response to Pastel's question. "Sister Thea is a little younger than I am. She had completed two years at a community college in Illinois, but had no idea what she wanted to do with her life. Sounds familiar, doesn't it? She tried substitute teaching, but found it unrewarding. Then she worked in assorted service-oriented jobs, all of which bored her. Finally, she went to see the priest at her church. He asked if she had ever considered a religious vocation. She shook her head."

"Almost a year passed, and Sister Thea still had no idea what she wanted to do. Meanwhile her grandmother died and left her a little money. Then her father suggested she see some of the world, so she decided to visit Greece. Her grandparents were born here. Like us, she came to Meteora and saw Agios Stefanos. The communal life of the monastery seemed very appealing. Before she departed, a young nun around Sister Thea's age recommended that she spend an hour in one of the private study areas not open to the public. After sitting alone for a while, she heard a soothing voice and sensed an invisible presence in the room. The voice assured her that everything she had experienced since leaving community college happened for a reason, that being to guide her to Agios Stefanos."

"That's quite a story," Sara responded. "You're not considering monastic life, are you?"

"I'm not a religious person, Sara. My parents are agnostics, and I never attended church in my youth. That's not to say that aspects of communal living aren't attractive, but having worked in a women's shelter, I learned how stressful it can be to interact with the same individuals day after day."

"Kind of like being on a cruise ship, isn't it?" Sara responded.

For the first time that day, Pastel laughed. Sara decided not to share her previous fears about Pastel falling to her death. "We'd better return to Simone before she starts to worry. I asked her to wait in the church."

Simone appeared to be napping when the pair reached the sanctuary. Pastel wondered if Sara thought Simone was ill or simply experiencing the normal effects of aging.

"Just because my eyes are closed doesn't mean I'm asleep," Simone announced. "I was thinking about my aunt, Pearl."

"What sparked that thought?" Sara inquired.

"I guess being in a church again. Aunt Pearl was very active in the Baptist church in our neighborhood. After my mother ran off to Europe and Pearl took me in, she insisted I attend services every Sunday. That's where I learned to sing. Aunt Pearl's church was a community of women not unlike this monastery. Many were divorced, widowed, or abandoned by men. They derived more strength, I suspect, from each other than from God."

As the three women left the sanctuary and descended the steps to the parking lot, Pastel told Simone about her conversation with Sister Thea. Simone expressed skepticism concerning the mysterious voice that Sister Thea had heard. "Given the dwindling population of nuns," Simone asserted, "I'll bet Sister Thea is in charge of identifying new recruits."

Mikail greeted his passengers warmly and admitted having worried that something bad happened to delay their return. Sara asked if they could stop somewhere for a light lunch before heading back to the Argonaut. Mikail recommended a pleasant taverna located near the place where they left the main highway.

At lunch the women split two orders of spanakopita, a large Greek salad with lots of feta cheese on top, and a bottle of assyrtiko wine. By the end of the meal, all three felt restored and slightly tipsy. Their pleasing buzz soon vanished, though, when Mikail got on the highway to Volos and encountered a massive traffic jam. He pulled out his cell phone, contacted his office, and learned that a large truck had swerved to avoid an automobile and gotten stuck in a ditch, blocking south-bound traffic.

For the next hour as Mikail inched along, all Sara could think about was missing the Argonaut's departure. When she arranged the excursion to Meteora privately, she was warned that the Argonaut's captain was under no obligation to delay departure if she was late returning to the ship.

The traffic jam eventually cleared and Mikail sped back to Volos, keeping one eye on the road and the other on the dashboard clock. Too nervous to sleep, his passengers watched the blur of scenery and hoped for the best. They reached the Argonaut's pier twelve minutes before the scheduled departure. Sara gave Mikail a substantial tip, for which he was effusively grateful. "Your visit to Agios Stefanos must have pleased God," he claimed.

"She took good care of us, didn't she?" Simone responded.

Once they boarded, Pastel left to check on her father and Simone sought the comfort of her bed for a nap before dinner. On the way to her room, Sara spotted a posted announcement. Brendan Greene, the ship's writer-in-residence, was sponsoring a writing contest on the day after tomorrow. Instructions for entrants would be available following tomorrow's visit to the island of Santorini. First prize was a chef's dinner for two in the Argonaut's private dining room. Sara planned to encourage Pastel to enter the contest.

When she entered her stateroom, Sara greeted the framed picture of David. She realized that the entire day had passed without her usual feelings of loneliness and regret. The companionship of Pastel and Simone was filling a void in Sara's life, and this awareness induced some feelings of guilt. The cruise was supposed to have been Sara's opportunity to reconnect with memories of her husband. She promised David that things would be different when the ship reached Sorrento, the first of several ports that the newlyweds had visited earlier on their honeymoon.

CHAPTER 7

SATURDAY, SEPTEMBER 17, 2022

When Sara arrived at the breakfast buffet, she saw Simone and Pastel sitting together. They beckoned for her to join them.

"I see you two also slept in this morning," Sara commented. As soon as she sat down, she raised her empty coffee cup to signal the server that coffee was needed immediately.

"There was no reason to get up early," Pastel replied. "Neither of us made any plans for today."

"I was going to call you after breakfast, so I'm glad I ran into you. Did you see the announcement about tomorrow's writing contest?"

"Dad told me about it. Right now, he's figuring out what he wants contestants to write about."

"Pastel, I think you should enter the competition," Sara declared. "You don't have to identify yourself. Your father won't know he's reading your submission."

"I agree with Sara," Simone chimed in. "You're clearly interested in becoming a writer. There's no time like the present to get started. What have you got to lose?"

"You're very considerate to think of me, but I'm clueless concerning what I'd write about. And what if Dad somehow found out? I don't need to get into another argument with him. Anyway, I know I wouldn't win. This cruise is full of highly educated individuals. In fact, the two of you should submit something. I'd love to read what you come up with."

Simone and Sara spent the rest of breakfast trying to convince Pastel to enter the writing contest. When they were unable to secure a commitment from their young friend, Simone proposed that the three of them take the tender to Santorini at noon and find a scenic place to have lunch. Sara liked the idea because she first wanted to visit the fitness center. Pastel had a massage scheduled for ten, but she agreed to be ready to go at noon.

The three women met on deck four at noon to catch the tender to Fira. Instead of her usual black outfit, Simone wore a dark green pleated skirt and yellow print blouse. Sara told her how stylish she looked. Sara opted for white pants and a boat-necked shirt with blue and white stripes. Both older women ribbed Pastel about having a boyfriend on Santorini because she wore a short navy skirt and snug, robin's egg blue tee shirt.

Boarding the tender was tricky due to choppy water. The tender constantly bounced up and down. Sara held Simone's hand to make sure she didn't trip. Despite a strong breeze, the threesome opted to sit outside where they could enjoy an unfettered view of Santorini. The island's population centers were located on cliffs hundreds of feet above the sea. As the tender approached land, Sara noticed cable car tracks running from the dock area up to Fira. As one cable car descended, the other made its way upward. Once the tender docked, Sara also spotted a paved walkway winding its way from the base of the cliffs to the town above.

"Well, girls, shall we try the cable car," Sara asked, "or walk up to Fira?"

"You must be joking," Simone replied. "That stairway at the monastery nearly did me in. I'm taking the cable car."

The threesome joined the line waiting to board the cable car. After two cars filled up ahead of them, they were able to catch the next car by squeezing in between a family with four young children and three crew members from the Argonaut. As the car crept up the cliffside, groaning under the weight of its human cargo, Simone admitted she might prefer to take the walkway back to the tender.

As they left the cable car station, Sara, Simone, and Pastel found themselves engulfed in a sea of tourists struggling to negotiate narrow streets filled on both sides with small shops and eateries. Pastel discovered an escape route and pulled her companions down an alley and into an area where taxis and tourist buses were parked. A clean-cut young man approached the trio and asked in broken English if they would like to find a less crowded place to visit. When Simone asked what he had in mind, he mentioned Oia, describing it as a charming village on the northwest tip of the island that locals call the pearl of Santorini. All three agreed that Oia sounded better than bustling Fira. The cost, split three ways, seemed reasonable. The young man said his name was Constantine and boasted that he was born in Santorini and wouldn't consider living anywhere else.

"Even Athens?" Pastel asked.

"You joke with Constantine, no? Athens is full of crooks, prostitutes, and politicians. Often can't tell the difference. Here in Santorini, all get along. Maybe it's the wine we make."

The deep blue Mediterranean was rarely out of sight during the drive to Oia. Clusters of white homes hugged the hills along the way. Occasionally a small roadside chapel appeared. Sara wondered about the fields of something in small clumps low to the ground. Constantine replied that they were grape vines and explained that the winds on Santorini could be so strong that grapes would be blown off typical upright vines.

When they reached Oia, Constantine parked in a large lot. The passengers were relieved to see only two large tourist buses nearby. Sara asked Constantine to recommend a restaurant overlooking the water. He knew just the place, a seafood bistro owned by two of his cousins.

"Do your cousins pay you to bring tourists to their place?" Simone asked.

"I get no euros," he responded with a grin, "but they give me all the calamari I want."

Sara thought Constantine was quite attractive and wondered if Pastel felt the same. Her young companion, she had noticed, rarely interacted with men her age on the ship. It was none of her business, of course, but being motherly came naturally to her. She thought it odd that a delightful young woman like Pastel should be so shy around her male peers.

Constantine guided the group through a maze of winding streets and alleys until they reached a fashionable pedestrian walkway with boutique shops on one side and bars and restaurants clinging to the cliffs on the other side. As they meandered along, Sara kept noticing photogenic scenes of interesting buildings bordered by beautiful flowers and backdropped by the sea. In her youth she would have wanted to paint them.

Eventually Constantine pointed to his cousins' bistro, perched precariously on the cliffside with the coastline spread out below. He told the three women the view from the patio was the best in all of Santorini, to which Simone responded "and also the scariest." Constantine assured her there had been no earthquakes "in years."

A short, bearded man wearing an apron called out from the patio, "Yahsoo! Tekahnis?"

Constantine announced, "Please meet my cousin, Nicholas. Looks like Zorba, no?"

Everyone laughed as Nicholas performed a few Greek dance steps before guiding his guests to a table overlooking the water. Before leaving, Constantine recommended the souvlaki, moussaka, and pastitsio. He warned the women not to accept any marriage proposals from his cousins and promised to return in an hour or so.

Sara ordered a bottle of local wine that Nicholas recommended. When he returned with the wine, Simone asked about the pastitsio. He explained it was the Greek version of lasagna, then added that Greeks probably invented lasagna.

"Is there anything Greeks didn't invent?" Simone asked.

Nicholas thought for a moment. "Minivans and texting."

Simone ordered a Greek salad, Pastel the moussaka, and Sara the pastitsio. Before Nicholas left, Pastel handed him her cell phone and asked for a photo of the threesome with their backs to the sea.

"You're retired," Sara said to Simone. "You sold your home. You aren't married."

Simone gave Sara a quizzical look, suggesting she had no idea where her friend was heading.

"Would you ever consider moving to a beautiful place like Santorini?"

"You mean like Louisa Durrell moving to Corfu?"

"Exactly, but without the family. You love Europe. Who knows, you might discover a fellow retiree in need of companionship."

"Like Louisa did?" Simone chuckled. "One was gay, one was a drunken sailor, and the other was married. Thanks, but no thanks. I've lived the life I chose. The time for a new chapter has passed."

Sara grew quiet at this point, while Pastel asked Simone about her favorite places to visit in Europe. What Simone had said about living the life she chose touched a nerve. "Is that what I've done?" Sara silently asked herself. "I chose to marry David instead of accepting a fellowship to study art in Paris. I chose to stop taking birth control pills because David wanted a family. I chose to stop teaching art and care for Mom when her Alzheimer's worsened. I never gave serious thought to making other choices. Wouldn't a circumspect person have considered other possibilities?"

"Are you all right?" Pastel asked Sara. "Nicholas wanted to know if you liked the wine he brought."

Sara apologized and told Nicholas that the wine was acceptable, but perhaps a bit too acidic for her. He offered to bring a different wine, one with a hint of sweetness. She declined, but Pastel wanted to try his alternative. When Nicholas returned with the wine, he was accompanied by his brother, Socrates, who juggled the women's lunch orders on both arms. Socrates took one look at Pastel and asked if she would marry him. Sara and Simone laughed, while Pastel turned crimson.

Constantine returned at three thirty, by which time the blend of sun, scenery, noisy neighbors, too much tasty food, and one too many wine refills had diminished conversation. All three women stared, trance-like, at their beautiful surroundings and inhaled the flower-perfumed air. When Constantine offered to show his customers several exclusive shops before returning to Fira, he was taken aback by their unanimous refusal. He professed having never been turned down for a shopping trip by women tourists.

"Don't all women desire to shop when they travel?" he asked.

"Young man," Simone responded, "you obviously do not understand the nature of true desire. Shopping is simply an option when there is nothing better to do. Where desire is involved, there are no options."

Constantine's puzzled look clearly indicated he had no idea what Simone meant. Sara and Pastel thanked Nicholas and Socrates for a lovely lunch and followed Constantine to his vehicle. The paving stones proved a challenge for Simone, so Sara once again held her hand.

Back on the Argonaut, the women decided to meet later at Gyorgy's bar. Sara planned to steep in a hot tub for a while before taking a cool shower. This combination had once been her prescription for re-invigorating herself after a busy day, but years had passed since she last indulged. When she entered her room, she saw David's photograph and said hello.

Relaxing in the tub, Sara wondered if David would have enjoyed visiting Meteora and Santorini. His love of political and economic history, she concluded, was unlikely to have been stimulated by either place. Most likely, in fact, he would have been bored. This thought led Sara to suspect that they probably would have disagreed over which excursions to undertake, had he lived to accompany her. The couple, however, rarely engaged in serious arguments. Sara attributed their domestic peace to her willingness to accede to David's wishes. These concessions, for the most part, did not bother her. Sara's practical nature dictated that a successful marriage required at least one spouse to be flexible.

The bath proved so relaxing that Sara actually dozed off. By the time she finished her cool shower and put on slacks and a tunic top, it was time to meet her friends. Sara was thankful she recently decided to have her hair cut short. David had preferred her hair long, which would have added another half hour to "getting ready" time.

Simone and Pastel already were seated at the bar when Sara arrived. She greeted Gyorgy and ordered an Old Fashioned.

"Are you tired of French chardonnay?" he asked. "Maybe you like to try Gyorgy's special? Called Man Overboard."

"It sounds very dangerous, Gyorgy. I promise to try one before the cruise is over."

Gyorgy asked the three women if they had met any men yet.

"You're the only man on this ship that we're interested in," Simone answered. Sara and Pastel nodded in agreement.

"I am very pleased, but do not tell my wife. She has many knives in the kitchen." Gyorgy wandered off to wait on other customers.

"I have something to tell you," Pastel announced. "I decided to enter the writing contest."

Sara and Simone expressed their delight over her change of heart and inquired about the writing assignment contestants had to complete.

"The essay must involve an interesting individual and be no longer than a thousand words."

"Someone you know?" Sara asked.

"It doesn't have to be."

"Believe me," Simone interjected, "you're much better off writing about someone you know. Not only will the writing be easier, but the finished product will sound more authentic."

"Other than my parents, you and Sara are the most interesting people I know," Pastel replied. "Naturally, I can't write about my parents if I want to remain anonymous."

"I'm not in Simone's league," Sara quickly added. "How

about it, Professor Baker. Will you help a writer in need?"

"How can I refuse? I've lived a reasonably long life compared to many African-Americans. If the essay is limited to a thousand words, that's less than four double-spaced pages."

"What you're saying is it's too brief an essay to encompass your entire life. What if I focus only on your time as a blues singer?"

"I like that idea," Sara chimed in. "How many teenage blues singers are there? Not many, I'd guess."

"If I'm to spend tomorrow writing about you," Pastel pointed out, "I'll need to gather information this evening. Can we move to someplace less noisy so I can take notes?"

Sara volunteered her room because it contained a sofa and two chairs. The women asked Gyorgy to prepare their free round of drinks in plastic cups. Pastel went to her room to fetch her laptop. The other two carried the drinks to Sara's room. When they entered, Simone noticed David's framed picture. Sara said it had been taken after David graduated from the University of Virginia. Simone snorted something about finding a better backdrop than a slaveholder's mansion.

When Pastel arrived, Sara offered a suggestion. "When I'm thinking about something that needs to be done, it helps me to create a visual picture. I've never really seen a blues singer give a live performance, and I'll bet Pastel hasn't either. Simone, can you describe what it was like for you?"

"You're asking me to travel back half a century. My memory isn't what it used to be, but I'll give it a try."

Pastel opened her laptop and readied herself to take notes. Sara relaxed on the sofa beside Simone and sipped her drink.

"Imagine a dimly lit nightclub full of tables," Simone began. "There's a small stage in the front of the place and a bar in the back. Clouds of cigarette smoke drift across the room. It's no wonder I got cancer."

"You got cancer?" Sara interrupted.

"What I meant to say is that it's a wonder I didn't get cancer.

The stage is just big enough for a few musicians and a singer. Tonight, the band consists of a guitarist, a bass player, a guy on tenor sax, and a drummer. The emcee is a fat black guy in a dark suit that's too small. He saunters up on stage and introduces the band members one by one. As he does, each musician riffs a bit on his instrument. They all wear black pants, white shirts open at the neck, and sunglasses. When the introductions are over, they play a warm-up number."

"Which one was the guy you were with?" Sara asked.

"The son of a bitch was the guitarist. He could make that thing talk, but that's about all he could do. Following the warm-up number, the bass player comes to the microphone and says, 'Now the person you've been waiting for. Ladies and gentlemen, please welcome Miss Simone Baker.'"

"The audience applauds. I delay my entrance for a minute or two to heighten the anticipation. The spotlight continues to focus on where I'm supposed to be. I slowly walk into the spotlight, which looks like a ship's beam in heavy fog. For a moment I look down at the individuals sitting near the stage. Then I move closer and single out a few women sitting beside men. I ask each woman, 'Miss, do you know the blues?' They respond, 'Sure do, honey. God knows I do. What woman don't know the blues?'"

"Then I look at the men sitting beside the women who just spoke. I ask them, 'Are you the reason your woman knows the blues?' Laughter erupts."

Pastel pleads for Simone to slow down a little so she can catch up on her notes.

"I move back a few steps and grip the microphone. All eyes are on me now. The chatter at the tables has died down. I say, 'You look at me and think, what's that sweet young thing know about the blues?' So let me tell you. I never knew my father. My mother abandoned me when I was young and ran off with some Jamaican dude to Europe. I went to live with my aunt. She took in laundry to keep food on our table. You still think I don't know the blues?"

"The audience answers my question. 'Child, you know the blues. Age don't matter.'"

"That's when I start singing 'I Got It Bad and That Ain't Good'." I start out real slow, like Billie Holliday used to do, so the audience can hear the angst in my voice. My goal when I sang the blues was to mesmerize people. I wanted them to feel the blues in an existential way because the blues are what unites us. Rich and poor. Black and white. We're all destined to suffer in some way."

Sara couldn't believe she was listening to the same woman who earlier seemed so frail and sickly. Talking about her past revealed an inner strength that belied Simone's physical presence. Sara easily visualized her friend captivating night club audiences.

Pastel recalled how Simone started singing in church, but she asked for additional background information. Simone said that Aunt Pearl loved listening to rhythm and blues groups on the radio. Because the lyrics often were bawdy, she didn't want Simone exposed to such music, but when her aunt wasn't at home, Simone tuned in a station out of Memphis and fell in love with the music. In high school, the music director heard her sing and insisted she try out for lead vocalist for the jazz band. She was selected. Members of a local blues group called the Blue Tones attended a high school performance, heard Simone sing, and invited her to join them. Aunt Pearl insisted, though, that she graduate first.

Simone's experience with the Blue Tones was wonderful at first. She fell for the guitarist, a guy named Buddy Short. Against her aunt's wishes, she married him. Despite his drug habit, they got along pretty well for a while, but then Simone was invited to audition in Memphis for Stax Records. Buddy and the other Blue Tones were not invited. Buddy demanded that Simone not go to the audition, and she told him to go to hell. He threatened to kill her if she went.

Aunt Pearl called the police, but they blew her off, saying that it sounded like a routine domestic spat. The police in those days rarely responded to complaints from blacks. The last straw was when Simone missed her period and thought she was pregnant. She told Buddy, and the next day he was gone for good. Turned out she wasn't pregnant after all. The band broke up. Aunt Pearl saw to it that the marriage was annulled and convinced Simone to apply to college. Based on her excellent high school record, she was accepted.

"Does that give you enough material to start your essay?" Simone asked. She seemed to be tired.

"I think so. I am so grateful to you."

"Then I shall take my leave. I haven't talked so much since I retired from teaching."

"Shall we have dinner?" Sara asked Pastel after Simone departed.

"I'd love to, but I need to go back to my room and think about how I'll organize my essay. Do you think I should use Simone's real name?"

"I wouldn't. She might not want the attention, especially with her feeling poorly. Before you go, though, I'd like to know why you changed your mind about entering the writing contest."

"When we returned from Santorini, I went back to my room to freshen up. When I looked in the mirror, I didn't see me as you now see me. I saw a woman with thinning gray hair, puffy circles under her eyes, wrinkled skin, and drooping breasts. She looked weary and woeful. I didn't hear a voice, as Sister Thea had at the monastery, but I knew that future vision of myself had to appear for a reason. I took it to be some kind of warning. I'll eventually grow old, so I'd better grow old doing what I want to do. Sounds weird, doesn't it?"

Sara grimaced. "Not weird at all, Pastel. Fact is, I see an aged face every time I look in a mirror. Until recently, I thought I was doing what I loved doing. Now, however, I'm not so sure. As long as my life was full of family and friends, there wasn't time to think about what was missing."

CHAPTER 8

SUNDAY, SEPTEMBER 18, 2022

The Argonaut was not scheduled to call at any port on Sunday because of the lengthy journey from Santorini to Sicily. Passengers were invited to take advantage of on-board activities, ranging from the writing contest and putting challenge to cooking lessons and wine tastings. Sara planned to work out at the fitness center, send emails to Marie and Randy, and take a cooking class on how to make crepes.

Arising an hour later than usual, Sara donned her workout outfit and went to the breakfast buffet. Pastel greeted her when she arrived and proudly showed her the completed registration form for the writing contest. The form was assigned a number so that Brendan Greene would not know who submitted entries. All essays had to be turned in to the ship's concierge by four o'clock that afternoon.

The winning essay, Pastel explained, would be announced at nine o'clock Monday morning, just before the Argonaut dropped anchor near the Sicilian city of Taormina. The prize for first place was a chef's dinner for two with premium wines. Sara congratulated Pastel once again for overcoming her reluctance to enter the contest. The young woman asked if Sara would mind looking over her essay before she submitted it. Simone would be a more informed critic, Sara suggested, but Pastel told her Simone needed to rest all day. Apparently, whatever was ailing her had gotten worse overnight.

After a healthy breakfast of two hard-boiled eggs, yogurt, and fruit, Sara jogged to the fitness center and once again discovered other passengers also had planned on exercising early in the day. After a ten-minute wait, a stationary bike became available. Sara climbed on and, against her better judgment, tuned into an international news program. The big story involved demonstrations in Iran over the death of a young woman who had been incarcerated by the so-called morality police for not wearing a head covering. As Sara saw it, the tragic incident was yet another example of the harm wrought by organized religion. Her parents refused to send her to church because they believed that much of the violence and killing in the world was a product of religious practices and animosities.

When Marie and Parker insisted on having Marcus baptized, it took all of Sara's willpower not to protest. Parker's parents were born-again Christians who Sara found over-bearing and self-righteous. It didn't help that they also were supporters of the ex-President. How they could reconcile their so-called Christian values with support for such an immoral and unethical individual was beyond her. On more than one occasion at a family gathering, Sara had to leave the room when Parker's mother started ranting about how liberals were ruining America. Just thinking about the woman caused Sara to up her bike's resistance and pedal faster.

Sara eventually moved on to the weight machines. When she and David used to exercise together on weekends, he frequently offered tips on how to develop her muscles. After she expressed concern that her arms were getting flabby, he advised lifting free weights. Marie accused her mother of being obsessed with exercise. As far as Sara was concerned, her daily workouts prevented her from becoming clinically depressed following David's tragic accident.

Once her workout was over, Sara showered and chose a colorful sleeveless dress to wear. She decided to check on her friend. Simone answered the door in her robe and nightgown. She seemed glad to see Sara and immediately asked how Pastel was doing.

"I saw her at breakfast this morning. She did register for the writing contest, so I imagine at this moment Pastel's waxing literary about your brief blues career."

Simone smiled. "She asked me to help with her essay, but I gave the excuse of needing to rest. She doesn't need my advice. It's important that the essay is the result of her own effort."

Sara admitted agreeing to read the completed essay before Pastel submitted it, but in light of Simone's comment, she vowed to limit any suggestions to grammatical matters. The two continued chatting for several minutes before Sara grew serious.

"I know I have no business prying into your private affairs, Simone, but I'm concerned about you. Yesterday when you told Pastel about the thick cigarette smoke when you used to sing, you mentioned something about cancer, then corrected yourself. Do you have cancer? Is that why you've been feeling poorly?"

Simone's formal persona softened slightly. "I guess my talent doesn't include lying. I was recently diagnosed with pancreatic cancer. For several months I'd been losing weight and feeling fatigued, but I figured it was either COVID or just part of the aging process. Then I started experiencing pain in my abdominal area. My doctor referred me to a specialist, and she ordered an MRI and blood tests. It turned out the cancer had advanced to the point where it could not be effectively eliminated."

Sara's eyes teared up as she reached for Simone's hand. "I'm so sorry, Simone. No wonder you've needed rest." Sara was at a loss regarding what else to say. It bothered her that she was unable to offer anything helpful or hopeful.

"I came into this world with the blues," Simone acknowledged with a sigh. "Looks like I'll be leaving it with the blues as well."

"Then let's make sure the time you have left is spent as enjoyably as possible."

"Baby, I'll drink to that," Simone responded with a wry laugh.

Before leaving, Sara promised to be Simone's companion for any excursions and activities she wished to undertake during the cruise. "You don't have to face your illness alone, Simone." Sara hugged her friend, being careful not to embrace too tightly. She could feel bones protruding from Simone's back.

On her way to the private lounge for passengers in more expensive state rooms, Sara thought about the value of friendships during times of illness and despair. Because David's death occurred at the onset of the Pandemic, she was denied direct contact with most of her close friends. Marie had to be both daughter and confidant, roles which she handled capably, though not always with the degree of compassion and empathy her mother desired. Sara wondered about the nuns at Agios Stefanos. Did they exhibit the kind of womanly understanding and caring that she craved in the aftermath of David's death or were they too preoccupied with their religious duties to focus on interpersonal relations?

Hannah Albright came to mind. Sara co-taught art with Hannah for two years before she left teaching to care for her mother. Hannah was a gifted watercolorist, a frustrating genre for young children to learn. While Sara worked on oil and acrylics with older students, Hannah nurtured the young ones and inspired them to produce many outstanding watercolor paintings. Hannah's relations with her own children, regrettably, were awful. Her teenage daughter actually reported Hannah to the school counselor, accusing her of neglect.

The private lounge provided access to computers and wi-fi connectivity. Sara intended to send emails to Marie and Randy, letting them know how she was enjoying the cruise. Randy's birthday was approaching, so she found a humorous on-line card of a young man getting patted down by a comely TSA agent. Sara was uncertain Randy would ever marry and settle down.

Sara had no problem writing to Randy, but Marie was a different matter. Still upset that Marie had announced her move just before Sara left on the cruise, she decided to direct her email to Marcus. Marie, of course, would have to read the email to her son. Sara described the Argonaut, its twelve decks, swimming pool, putting green, and kitchen for cooking classes. After mentioning some of the places the ship would visit, she expressed the hope that her grandson one day would go on a cruise. The email ended with "Your loving Nana" and a smiling emoji.

Once she pressed the "send" key, Sara felt guilty about investing so little time in composing the two messages. When she and David used to go away, David took responsibility for communicating with the children. His messages were always clever. Often, they took the form of a game in which Marie and Randy had to guess where their parents were and what they were doing. The clues he provided typically were very funny.

Seeing that it was almost time for the cooking class, Sara went to her room to change into clothes that she didn't mind getting messy. Once she arrived at the classroom and discovered she was paired with an attractive middle-aged man, however, she regretted this decision. He was slender and a little taller than Sara with neatly combed gray hair and brilliant blue-green eyes. He wore stylish linen pants and a green cashmere sweater.

While they waited for the instructor to arrive, Sara's partner introduced himself. "My name is Trevor Collins. Allow me to apologize in advance for what shortly will become obvious. I am totally lacking in culinary expertise. I am relieved to see that you wisely chose to wear more appropriate attire for cooking."

Sara felt her face redden. "I'm Sara Castle. I only dress this way because I enjoy spilling things. I'll try my best not to spill anything on you."

Sara surveyed the room. There were twelve cooking stations, each equipped with a stove top, small sink, assorted cooking utensils, several pans, a cutting board, paper towels, and four plates. Of the twenty-four participants, only two were men. Having recently spent so much time in the company of Pastel and Simone, Sara looked forward to cooking crepes with Trevor.

Assistants began to distribute ingredients for making crepes as Chef Jayat welcomed the participants. She asked how many had made crepes before, and nine hands were raised. Sara and Trevor did not raise their hands. Chef Jayat explained that step one involved making the batter. Instructions were given along with warnings about not leaving lumps in the batter. When the batter was made, it needed to sit for a while. During that time, wine would be served and participants needed to decide what fillings or toppings they desired for their crepes. Once the batter was ready, the chef planned to demonstrate "the art of crepe-making." Sara appreciated the reference to cooking as an art form.

The next hour and a half went by quickly, too quickly for Sara. She thoroughly enjoyed making a mess of her cooking station with Trevor. Both requested refills of wine. Once the batter was ready, Sara heated a small amount of oil in the special crepe pan and Trevor poured in the batter. Sara swirled it until the batter was evenly distributed around the pan. After the batter browned slightly, Trevor picked up the spatula and attempted to lift the thin crepe and flip it over. Three tries were required before he succeeded, by which time both cooks were laughing so hard they were crying. Trevor insisted more wine was required to perform the delicate task of flipping the crepe. Chef Jayat suggested that perhaps the gentleman might have more success flipping burgers at McDonalds. The entire room exploded in laughter.

Trevor eventually got the hang of flipping crepes, so Sara took a turn. She had no difficulty, earning her a "bon" from Chef Jayat. More wine was served as the participants consumed their crepes and got to know each other. Sara learned that Trevor was a widower and a recently retired architect living in Tennessee. She mentioned her experience teaching art in elementary school and her two grown children. Just as Sara was about to share the fact that she lost her husband, she noticed the time and recalled promising to review Pastel's essay before it was submitted.

As Sara departed, Trevor asked if she would meet him for a drink that evening. Only after she accepted his invitation and went to the coffee bar to meet Pastel did she remember her daughter's warning about single men on cruises who preyed on unaccompanied women. She decided to trust her instincts about Trevor.

Pastel had a latte waiting for Sara. She could tell her young friend was nervous as she handed over a copy of her essay. Pastel avoided eye contact, and her hand was shaking. The essay was entitled "Miss B. and the Blues." Instead of an author, the heading was the number eleven.

Sara nodded approvingly as she read the essay. When she got to the last lines, she read them twice to herself, then aloud a third time.

"When it came to the blues, Miss B. was no spectator. Despite her youth, she had lived the blues. Perhaps you are wondering why she also chose to sing the blues. Here's what I think. Singing the blues brought Miss B. pleasure, the pleasure that comes from feeling connected to others who have experienced hardship, heartache, and loss."

"Pastel, this is beautiful," Sara said enthusiastically. "I can just see Simone standing in that smoke-filled room captivating her audience. You're an artist with words, my dear."

Pastel wiped her eyes with a napkin. "You are so encouraging. I'll bet you were a wonderful art teacher."

Sara returned the essay and wished Pastel good luck. She wanted to tell her about cooking class and Trevor, but Pastel was anxious to turn in her essay before four o'clock. The two agreed to meet later at the bar. Sara then remembered agreeing to meet Trevor for a drink. Now she could find out what Pastel thought about her cooking companion.

Sipping her latte, Sara reflected on Pastel's comment about

her being a wonderful art teacher. At the risk of seeming boastful, Sara indeed felt she was a very capable art instructor. Students were always excited to attend her classes. The work they produced made her proud and elicited praise from observers. Did she still possess the stamina and motivation to teach art to young people? A decade had passed since she last taught.

When she returned to her room, Sara considered what to wear that evening. Trevor had joked about her cooking outfit. Now she intended to show him a more glamorous Sara Castle. After laying out several possible ensembles, she selected a simple, never-out-of-style black dress with a modest v-cut decolletage revealing just a hint of cleavage. With a vibrant Hermes scarf wrapped around her neck, she'd be the picture of tasteful elegance. Looking at herself in the mirror, Sara smiled approvingly. David used to embarrass her at parties by referring to her as his trophy wife. After this happened several times, she began to joke that David was her trophy husband, the kind of trophy you mount on the wall.

Sara and Pastel arrived at the bar within minutes of each other. Sara informed Gyorgy that the drinks were on her tonight because Pastel had written a beautiful essay for the writing contest. Given the stress of completing her entry, Pastel agreed that a drink was exactly what she needed.

As Gyorgy prepared Pastel's Cosmopolitan, he said, "You know, my father owned a small vineyard. He used to say people are like grapes. Both need to be stressed to realize potential."

"Do you really believe that's true, Gyorgy?" Sara asked.

"My father always spoke the truth, except to my mother."

"I see I'm late for the party," Trevor called out as he took a seat next to Sara.

"Let me introduce my co-chef, Trevor Collins," Sara said to Pastel and Gyorgy.

"You are making Gyorgy very jealous," the bartender replied.

"Well, I hope you are making Trevor a Manhattan," Trevor responded with a wink.

For the next half hour, Sara, Pastel, and Trevor exchanged bits of personal information. Sara asked if Trevor's wife had been ill for a long time before she passed away. Trevor answered that Ava did not die from disease. She was a foreign correspondent on assignment in Haiti when she was shot and killed by a gang member. The assailant, according to Trevor, was never apprehended.

Trevor learned that Sara's husband also had died unexpectedly just before the Pandemic began. Taking the cruise was her way of fulfilling his wish for them to go on a second honeymoon. Sara told her companions about her children, Marie and Randy, and her grandson, Marcus. Trevor and Ava did not have any children. Whether he regretted being childless was not discussed.

Pastel told Trevor that she came on the cruise to accompany her father, who needed a wheelchair because of rheumatoid arthritis. The cruise line invited him to be the Argonaut's writer-in-residence. Pastel said her mother was a well-known artist and currently separated from her father. Sara added that Pastel submitted an essay for her father's writing contest. Trevor considered entering the contest as well, but decided he didn't want to embarrass himself. Hearing this, Sara turned to Pastel and said with a grin, "Trevor did a pretty good job of that trying to flip crepes this afternoon."

The jazz band started to play, making further conversation difficult. After listening for a while, the three bar-mates wandered off to the deck below and walked outside. The cool evening air felt invigorating. Pastel eventually excused herself in order to check on how her father was coming along with the writing contest entries.

Sara and Trevor continued strolling around the ship. Trevor said how much he enjoyed the cooking lesson and getting together in the bar. It had been difficult, he admitted, to resume any semblance of a social life after Ava was killed. The ship's captain passed the pair at one point and commented on how they made a lovely couple. Sara didn't know what to say. Apparently neither did Trevor because he just smiled.

When Sara's arms began to develop goosebumps from the cool air, Trevor suggested they go inside. "I know we've just met," he said, "but how would you feel about attending tonight's dance with me? If you think I'm hilarious at flipping crepes, just wait until you see me dance."

The way Trevor was comfortable making fun of himself was pleasing to Sara. Based on first impressions, she liked him. Nonetheless, being asked on a date by someone other than David had not occurred in over three decades. Trevor's invitation caused her to feel things she hadn't felt in many years. Following an embarrassing silence, she responded, "I haven't danced in a long time. I'm not even sure I remember how. Besides, I'm not used to staying up late. If you'll excuse me, I need to check on my friend, Simone. She's not feeling very well."

Trevor looked at her, but did not immediately reply. Finally, he offered a benign smile and expressed what really was on Sara's mind. "You don't feel it's right to go dancing with me, do you? This trip was supposed to be your second honeymoon with David. I understand completely, and I promise not to bother you again."

Trevor left Sara staring at the sea and thinking, "Believe me, it really wasn't a bother."

CHAPTER 9

MONDAY, SEPTEMBER 19, 2022

Thanks to persistent night sweats, or perhaps meeting Trevor, Sara got very little sleep. She tossed and turned for hours, eventually getting out of bed feeling exhausted. Pulling back the curtains for the sliding door to her veranda, Sara was treated to a view of the brooding slopes of Mount Etna silhouetted against the dawning sky. Soon the Argonaut would drop anchor off the coast of Taormina. A photograph or two might have been nice, but all she wanted to do at that moment was cool off in the shower.

Feeling revived after the shower, Sara called Simone to see if she wanted to have breakfast. For a change, Simone sounded upbeat. She suggested meeting at the outdoor café near the swimming pool. Over dark roast coffee and Italian pastry, the two women discussed Pastel. Sara acknowledged being impressed by the young woman's essay, and Simone responded that she looked forward to reading it. What she said next, however, struck Sara as odd.

"I understand that Pastel is excited about pursuing her interest in becoming a writer, but there's more to the process than entering a writing contest." Simone hailed a passing server and requested more coffee. "I don't think she has any idea what she's getting into."

"Don't you believe having a famous writer for a father has given her some insight into the challenges of writing for a living?"

Simone sipped her coffee. "She only has known her father since he already was an established and well-regarded author. What came before is what I'm talking about. I'm sure there were years when young Brendan Greene grappled with finding his true voice. While most folks get on with their lives, young writers frequently remain stuck in neutral while they try to harness discontent and convert it to compelling prose. Do you understand what I'm saying?"

"Sounds like you're worried that Pastel might jump into writing before she understands who she really is."

"Yes, that's what I'm saying."

"Do we ever understand who we really are?" Sara asked.

"Good morning, ladies. You two appear to be having a serious conversation."

Sara and Simone turned to see Pastel. "We were just finishing breakfast," Sara responded. "Are you excited about finding out who won the writing contest?"

"Excited and nervous. Dad is wheeling his way with an armful of essays to the lounge on deck twelve."

"Then let us be off," Simone announced.

Sara and Pastel dropped Simone off at the elevator and walked up the main staircase to the lounge. A small crowd had already assembled when they arrived. Pastel chose to remain at the back of the group where her father couldn't see her, but Sara moved forward. Brendan Greene soon rolled in and parked his wheelchair behind a long table. Next to him stood the Argonaut's activity director, Heather McKay, and Chef Jayat.

Heather called the gathering to order. "It's grand to see such a good turnout. Our writer-in-residence, the renowned Brendan Greene, has informed me that twenty-nine budding literary lions submitted essays for the writing contest. As you know, our talented Chef Jayat generously consented to reward today's winner and a companion of his or her choice with a very special dinner this evening. Now, it is my sincere pleasure to introduce the three-time winner of the Fitzgerald Literature Prize, Brendan Greene."

"Thank you, Heather, and thanks to all of you who submitted your essays. I thoroughly enjoyed reading about the special in-dividuals you chose to focus on. Based on what I read, we have some very promising authors on the Argonaut. It is a shame only one award can be given." Greene picked up the essay that topped the pile of papers and surveyed the audience. With a gleam in his eye, he said, "I haven't been this excited since my daughter, Pastel, was born."

Sara looked back and saw Simone squeezing Pastel's hand. Did Brendan know that his daughter had entered the contest? she wondered.

"Now, the moment you've been waiting for. My selection for the best essay is submission number eleven. Would the author please come forward."

A muffled cry of delight could be heard from the rear of the audience. "It sounds like the winner is present," Greene said as he craned his neck to see who it was. "And I'm guessing by the expression of surprise that the winner is not a man." Everyone laughed as Pastel made her way to the front.

A look of shock crossed Greene's face when he saw who the winner was. "Can this really be true?" he exclaimed. "I have chosen my own daughter's essay. Let me assure you, this contest was not rigged. I had no idea Pastel submitted an essay, and I am very embarrassed. No name appeared on any of the submissions."

Murmurs among the crowd implied that many were skeptical about Greene's assurances.

Pastel stepped forward and addressed the group. "My father is telling the truth. He had no idea I entered the contest. Years ago, in fact, he discouraged me from ever becoming a writer. I know he is as surprised as I am. I never believed I had a chance of winning. Don't get me wrong. I'm gratified to have won. You cannot know how much it means to me to have been chosen by the person who never wanted me to follow in his footsteps. Still, I must respectfully decline the prize. Believe me, a special dinner by Chef Jayat is very hard to turn down."

Pastel's withdrawal drew applause from the crowd. Brendan thanked his daughter for being so gracious and reached for the second-place submission. "I should tell you that the first and second place entries were very close in my scoring. I was awarded a maximum of twenty-five points for each of four categories: characterization, organization, grammar, and word usage. The second-place paper was only two points behind the first-place paper. Chef Jayat's dinner for two belongs to submission number sixteen.

A young man of average height with wire-rim glasses and jet-black hair pulled back in a man-bun embraced the older couple with whom he was standing and came forward. He introduced himself to Brendan Greene, and they shook hands. Sara guessed he was in his late twenties or early thirties and that the older couple were his parents.

"I have the pleasure of awarding the prize to Damian Diaz," Greene announced. "Mr. Diaz wrote about his grandmother's experiences immigrating to the United States."

"My mother's mother meant the world to me," the young man said. His voice broke as he added, "I only wish she were here today." Diaz turned to Chef Jayat and said something inaudible, then approached Pastel and asked, "Would it be presumptuous of me, Miss Greene, to ask you to share the prize with me?" The audience clapped. Pastel blushed.

Brendan Greene said, "A noble gesture, Mr. Diaz."

Sara couldn't make out what Pastel said to Damian. The crowd began to disperse, while Sara and Simone waited for Pastel to finish chatting with the young man. After a few minutes, Damian departed with the older couple and Pastel walked over to her friends.

"Congratulations, Pastel. You must be so proud." Sara gave her a big hug.

"I don't care about the prize. Just knowing Dad judged my essay to be worthy of winning was reward enough."

"Nonetheless, you deserve to share the special dinner," Simone asserted. "It's a win-win. You know you finished in first place and you get to enjoy the company of a handsome young man for dinner."

"I didn't accept Damian's dinner invitation. At least not yet. I told him I'd think about it."

"The dinner's tonight, Pastel. What have you got to lose?" Sara sounded incredulous.

"You and Simone don't understand," Pastel replied as she slipped away from where her father was chatting with several admirers. "I haven't been alone with a man my age in a long time."

"You weren't just an employee in that women's shelter, were you?" Simone asked knowingly.

Pastel looked surprised. "How did you know? Not even my father and mother know."

"Let's just call it the intuition of a woman who has experienced mistreatment by a man, but listen to me. You can't allow that bad experience, however painful, to prevent you from living your life. You need to notify Mr. Diaz that you would be pleased to join him for dinner. You're not agreeing to marry the guy. It's just dinner, Pastel, and a fine one at that."

"Simone's right, Pastel. Damian seems like a well-mannered and thoughtful young man."

"So did Jeremy, the guy who beat me up and then stalked me."

Sara put her arm around Pastel's shoulder. "Please don't allow Jeremy to control your life."

The three women left the lounge to get coffee and continue their discussion. Pastel left Damian a message saying she would like to attend the chef's dinner with him. Sara asked her two companions if they wanted to visit Taormina with her, but both declined. Simone said she promised to give Pastel feedback on her essay and discuss the challenges of becoming a writer. First, however, she intended to watch Queen Elizabeth's funeral on television.

"What a remarkable person she turned out to be," Sara responded.

"Just so you know, I think both of you are pretty remarkable as well," Pastel added.

Sara left her companions to inquire about things to see and do in Taormina. The activity director announced that the Argonaut was ready to drop anchor off Giardini Naxos. The tender ride to shore would take about twenty minutes.

When she reached the concierge's desk, Sara expressed her desire to visit places with impressive works of art. The concierge, a middle-aged woman who spoke English with an Eastern European accent, smiled and said the entire town was a work of art. Well-known artists, composers, writers, and actors had been spending time in Taormina since the early nineteenth century because of its natural beauty.

Sara asked if there was an art museum in Taormina. The concierge mentioned the Sicilian Museum of Art and Popular Traditions in Palazzo Corvaja, but she advised Sara to spend her time wandering through town and enjoying the historical sites and cafes.

"Rather than hanging around lots of dead artists, why not experience a place alive with the cultures of Greece, Rome, the Middle East, France, Spain, and Italy?" she asked.

Sara felt like telling the woman there would be no cultures without dead artists of various kinds, but she was anxious to get off the ship, so she thanked her and went back to the room to change into shorts, a sleeveless top, and comfortable walking shoes.

After checking on the Argonaut's departure time, Sara caught a tender that bobbed up and down in choppy water until it reached port. There she found an assortment of tour buses headed for Taormina and Mount Etna. When she used to travel with David, he always insisted on having a plan before they set out to do some sightseeing. Today she possessed no specific plan, but instead of feeling uneasy, she actually felt liberated. Even her original notion of spending time in an art museum seemed too constraining. Sara couldn't remember the last time she just wandered around a new place. Wasn't that what adventure was all about? Maybe the concierge was on to something. Sara was free to do whatever she wanted to do. She wasn't even sorry that Simone and Pastel had chosen to remain on the ship.

Sara scanned her surroundings and noticed groups of people, some in bathing suits, others carrying coolers and baskets, heading past the bus parking lot to the beach beyond. The temperature, she guessed, had to be almost ninety degrees. "Do I really want to hop on a bus, ride to town, and walk around in this heat?" she asked herself. The notion of spending time on the beach and swimming in the sea seemed far more appealing. Joining the parade of beachgoers, Sara started making a mental list of the items she'd need to purchase. After walking several hundred yards, she spotted vendors selling various beach-related paraphernalia. Her belt bag fortunately contained plenty of euros. Using a credit card in strange places, as David frequently had reminded her, was inviting trouble.

Sara's mini-buying spree yielded a beach towel big enough to stretch out on, a pair of cheap flip-flops to protect her feet from the hot sand, a container of sunscreen spray, and bottled water. She considered buying a tee shirt to wear in the water, but noticed that many women on the beach were topless. "Who do I know here? Nobody. What difference does it make if I don't wear a top? I'm not ashamed of my body."

Sara took off her shoes and slipped on the flip-flops, sprayed herself with sunscreen, and strolled to the far end of the beach. There were few families with young children around. Sara was glad because she didn't want her beach time spoiled by lots of noisy, over-active youngsters. The blue-green water looked so inviting she decided to get wet immediately. After spreading her beach towel and anchoring it with her other possessions, she removed her sleeveless top. For a second, she debated whether or not to keep her bra on. Then she unhooked it and left it on the beach towel. Sara considered sending a selfie of her liberated breasts to Marie, but realized she left her cell phone on the ship.

As she entered the water, a wave of nostalgia washed over her. The current, adventuresome version of Serenity Sunshine Castle, she realized, was also the person with whom David had fallen in love. Thirty years of child-rearing, household management, teaching, caring for her mother, and providing emotional support for David had diminished the adventuresome version considerably, but in this moment, topless in Giardini Bay, Sara understood that some vestige of the former Serenity still survived.

After admiring the cliff-crusted coastline as well as several generously muscled young men, Sara walked out to a point where her feet barely touched bottom and began swimming parallel to the shore. The farther she swam, the more detached from reality she felt. It occurred to her that she was approaching a transcendent state of grace in which the desperate thoughts she had entertained when she decided to complete the second honeymoon journey could be set aside, at least for the moment.

Pausing her swim and looking around, Sara suddenly became aware of having gone out too far from shore. As she headed back to the beach, she reckoned that drowning off the Sicilian coast failed to meet her standard for a fitting end to life. If she were going to die on her second honeymoon, at least it should be in a place that she and David had visited together on their original honeymoon. Not until the Argonaut reached Sorrento would Sara be back in familiar territory.

Reaching the shore exhausted from swimming, Sara stretched out on the beach towel and allowed her body to recuperate and soak up the sun's rays. After ten minutes on her stomach, she rolled over on her back. That's when she heard someone say, "Sara, what a pleasant and unexpected surprise."

Looking up, she saw the trim figure of Trevor Collins in a Hawaiian print swimsuit and sandals. That he spent lots of time in the sun was obvious. While the upper halves of his arms and legs were pink, the lower halves were brown. Remembering that she was topless, Sara's first instinct was to reach for her sleeveless top, but she quickly decided it didn't matter if Trevor saw her au naturel.

"You're welcome to join me, but I only have one beach towel," she said.

Trevor thanked her and replied that he was going to purchase a towel of his own. When he returned with the towel, he also had brought two white wine spritzers. Trevor spread out his towel and sat while Sara informed him of Pastel's first place finish in the writing contest. The conversation turned to youthful ambitions. Sara admitted having wanted to become a famous artist. Trevor's early ambition was to play golf on the professional circuit.

"I know you were an architect," Sara replied. "Were you also able to become a pro golfer?"

"Sadly, that ambition, like yours, was not achieved. Perhaps dreams are overrated."

When the wine spritzers were finished, Sara and Trevor agreed they had enough sun for the day. He suggested catching a hop-on bus into Taormina and visiting the amphitheater. Sara was reminded of her late husband who preferred historical sites to art museums. Trevor even resembled David. Both men were tall, sandy-haired, and broad-shouldered. They carried themselves with a similar air of self-assurance and felt at ease in social situations.

Addressing Trevor's recommendation to see the amphitheater, Sara lied and responded, "Since I've never been to Taormina, one tourist attraction is as good as another."

On the way to the bus, Sara purchased a straw bag to hold her beach towel and other items. David bought a linen shirt to wear over his tee shirt and a cap with the logo of an Italian soccer team. They caught a bus to town and were relieved to find it air conditioned. Both complained of being sun-burned.

The bus dropped them off near the amphitheater. It didn't take long in the midday sun for both individuals to admit having had enough of the intense heat. Sara suggested finding a cozy café in a shaded location. After passing several crowded establishments, they turned down a side street and discovered a secluded bistro with a courtyard shielded from the sun by several ancient olive trees.

After ordering cold beers and calzones, Sara and Trevor picked up where they left off on the beach. She wondered why he seemed disappointed about pursuing architecture instead of golf. He admitted not achieving the recognition he hoped for as an architect and acknowledged it was too late to rectify the situation. Sara wanted to admit she shared similar feelings of disappointment, but hesitated for fear of appearing to be unthankful for having raised two wonderful children and a delightful grandson.

The two went on to discuss the advantages and disadvantages of being alone. When Trevor's wife, Ava, was alive, he constantly worried that harm would befall her while on assignment abroad. Sara admitted that David frequently was so preoccupied with courting potential donors that he seemed, even when at home, to be distant and distracted. Trevor and Sara went on to offer examples of special times with their spouses when everything clicked and they realized why they married them.

The opportunity to discuss meaningful matters with another person who had experienced profound and unexpected loss meant a great deal to Sara. When she tried to shift the conversation from the past and the present to the future, however, Trevor grew quiet. She had an inkling why, but decided not to probe further. Besides, the time had come to head back to port and catch a tender to the Argonaut.

Not much was said on the return journey. Upon reaching the ship and completing the check-in process, Trevor thanked Sara for a pleasant day ashore and departed. She hoped her attempt to find out what the future held for Trevor had not offended him.

All Sara wanted to do was shower off the sand that stuck to her sunscreen and irritated her bodily crevasses. By the time she finished bathing, shaving her legs, and applying lotion to her dry skin, the time for two-for-one drinks with Gyorgy was almost over. Sara rushed to the bar and found Simone nursing a Manhattan.

Gyorgy greeted her with a smile. "I was worrying you had abandoned me. I make two drinks now before the end of two-for-one time."

"You are so kind, Gyorgy. How about two Old Fashioneds?"

"You are too young for Old Fashioned, but I will make it anyway."

"How was Taormina?" Simone asked.

Sara related her decision to hang out at the beach and go topless. She also mentioned meeting Trevor and having lunch in Taormina.

"Sounds like you're getting some of that adventure you've been craving. Bravo for baring your breasts. What was it like to be with Trevor for the day?"

"He's a perfect gentleman, but a bit of an enigma. There's a deep sadness about him that goes beyond losing his wife so tragically. I couldn't get him to talk about what the future might hold."

"Men can be that way, though my personal experience in that regard is rather limited. I believe they relish being hard to figure out. I met with Pastel and enjoyed reading what she wrote about me. The girl has talent. I just hope she has some idea of what she's getting into. Winning a shipboard writing contest is one thing. Becoming a published author is altogether different. You need a stout ego to tolerate rejection after rejection on your way to building a reputation."

"It was good of you to spend some time with Pastel, especially since I know you're not feeling well." Sara finished her first Old Fashioned and grabbed a handful of potato chips. "If I may ask, what's been the hardest part of dealing with your cancer?"

Simone responded immediately. "Learning to live without hope."

"Perhaps that's what Pastel needs to do if she wants to be a writer," Sara replied. Her thoughts turned to the young Syrian woman she met in Xanthi. "Is living without hope the same as living without a future?" she asked herself.

CHAPTER 10

SATURDAY, SEPTEMBER 20, 2022

Sara was in the midst of painting a full-length portrait of an unclothed Trevor Collins when her cell phone buzzed, startling her awake. She reached for the phone fearing it might be Marie.

"Who is it?"

"You sound strange. Are you okay?"

Sara struggled to identify the voice, but she still was groggy. "Pastel, is that you?"

"I've obviously awakened you, haven't I? I'm so sorry, Sara."

"Don't worry. I was having the strangest dream. Is everything alright?"

"More than all right. Damian and I had a lovely time at the chef's dinner last night. We decided, in fact, to rent a car today when we reached Sorrento and drove to Pompeii. We were wondering, actually I was wondering, if you and Simone would join us."

Fully alert now, Sara guessed that Pastel was excited to take an excursion with Damian, but still uncertain about being alone in a foreign country with a man she just met. "In other words," Sara chuckled, "you wouldn't mind a couple of chaperones."

"Shouldn't prudence trump infatuation?" Pastel asked in a lighthearted way.

"Probably not a bad idea."

"Can you check with Simone about joining us?"

"I'll be glad to. When and where should we meet?"

"Let's meet in the departure lounge after the announcement that the ship has reached port. I've been told we need to take a tender like we did in Santorini."

Sara put down her cell phone and collected her thoughts. She had looked forward to exploring Pompeii on her own and reconnecting with memories of her visit with David, but Pastel's request aroused Sara's motherly instincts. The young woman was right to invite her friends. Marie might no longer require Sara's assistance, but it was comforting to know someone needed her.

Sara phoned Simone, hoping she was awake by now. When her friend answered, Sara apologized for calling so early and explained Pastel's request.

"Under normal circumstances I'd love to join you and see the ruins of Pompeii, but I'm something of a ruin myself at the moment. I need to save what little energy I have for Rome tomorrow. I'm really glad you called, however. I was going to ask you to go with me to Rome after we've docked at Civitavecchia."

Once again, Sara faced the choice between helping a friend and having some alone time with David, or at least with memories of David.

When Sara paused before responding, Simone added, "If you've got other plans, I'll be fine on my own, Sara. There's someone I need to see in Rome, and I know the Eternal City can become the Infernal City if you get lost."

If Simone was willing to brave the traffic and congestion of Rome on her own in order to visit someone, that someone had to be pretty important. As sickly as her friend was, Sara couldn't allow her to go alone. Besides, her curiosity had been whetted. Who was this mysterious person?

"I'd love to accompany you to Rome," Sara answered. "Let's meet this evening at the bar to discuss travel details."

Sara ordered breakfast from room service and showered while

waiting for it to be delivered. Given the persistent heat wave across southern Europe and the uneven surfaces in Pompeii, she decided to wear Bermuda shorts, a top that screened out ultraviolet rays, and sturdy running shoes. When she and David visited the ruins, the steady rain made walking extremely challenging. On several occasions, Sara tripped and fell on the wet paving stones. The bruises on her legs became conversation pieces when she returned home.

After breakfast Sara found her companions waiting in line to catch the tender to Sorrento. Sara inquired about their award dinner last night. Pastel and Damian told her the dinner was "awesome," "epic," and "amazing." Sara was all too familiar with the younger generation's overused terms because Marie frequently relied on them. David used to encourage his daughter to broaden her vocabulary by using more descriptive words, but she usually dismissed his advice with a terse, "Whatever." Sara persisted in her quest for more details about the dinner and eventually learned the couple enjoyed puff pastry and tomato appetizers, elegant braised short ribs in cabernet sauce, acorn squash puree with butter and brown sugar, and tropical fruit salad. An assortment of French wines complimented the meal.

The tender ride thankfully was brief. Damian's long legs were folded up so tightly that his knees almost touched his chest. Once on shore the trio located the car rental agency and once again waited in line. It was nearly eleven by the time the paperwork was completed and the three tourists were escorted to their rental, a late model Toyota Camry. The rental agent informed them the drive to Pompeii was approximately seventeen miles, but they should allow at least an hour because of heavy traffic and frequent switchbacks. Her last words were to stay alert for signs to Pompeii because the turn-off was easy to miss.

Damian volunteered to drive, and neither woman protested. David almost always drove when he and Sara traveled anywhere. Pastel suggested that Sara sit in the front passenger's seat since her legs were longer. Once on the road, Sara decided to learn more about Damian's background.

"Were those your parents I saw hugging you when Brendan Greene announced that you won the writing contest?" she asked.

"How'd you guess?" Damian replied with a grin. "They insisted I accompany them on the cruise because they're worried, I'm not gyroscopic enough where my life is concerned."

"Gyroscopic?" Sara asked.

"It's my dad's term. He was trained as an engineer. Gyroscopes help keep ships balanced and stabilized so they don't rock too much. My parents believe I spend too much time working and not enough time playing."

"Sounds like you've got some pretty wise parents," Sara responded. "What is it that keeps you so busy working?"

Pastel interrupted at this point. "Damian's working on a doctorate in Latin American Studies at the University of Texas. He wants to be a professor." The young woman sounded very impressed.

"How far along with your studies are you?"

"I'm at the point where I need to form my dissertation committee. Once we can agree on my topic, I'm probably looking at another three years."

Sara patted Damian on the shoulder. "I met David, my husband, when I was an undergraduate and he was in graduate school. I saw how hard he worked on his dissertation. You'll be glad when the process is finished, I'm sure."

Damian asked Sara what she and David studied at the university and what they were doing now. He quickly apologized when Pastel told him that David had been killed in a traffic accident. Sara went on to say that David studied political science and economics, while she majored in art and art history. She asked Damian about his parents, and he said they owned a group of Tex-Mex restaurants in the Austin area. His pride in how they started with a secondhand food truck and built a thriving chain of eateries was evident.

Sara began chatting about her honeymoon visit with David to Pompeii when Damian slapped the steering wheel and became visibly agitated.

"I think I just missed the turn-off for Pompeii. If I'm not mistaken, we're now headed for Naples." He continued muttering to himself about not paying attention to road signs. Pastel tried to calm him, pointing out that driving in Italy could be confusing. He insisted, though, on blaming himself for not checking directions on-line before they started.

It was past noon when the group finally reached Pompeii and parked the car. The fact that Damian kept apologizing for missing the correct turn left Sara with the impression he was a high-strung perfectionist and very hard on himself. These were characteristics, she believed, that Pastel probably could relate to. Sara offered to treat her friends to a glass of wine before they entered the famous World Heritage site, but they opted for espresso instead. Sara thought to herself, "All Damian needs right now is espresso so he can get really wired. Wine would have calmed him down."

Everyone visited the restroom before getting coffee and biscotti. Sara purchased a floppy hat to protect her face and neck. Despite using suntan lotion, these areas got burned the previous day at the beach.

Once inside the enormous excavation area, Sara suggested that Pastel and Damian go ahead of her as she wished to proceed more slowly and reimagine special moments she and David had shared on their visit. Pastel recommended they all meet at the entrance gate at four o'clock. That would allow ample time to return to Sorrento, drop off the rental car, perhaps grab a lemoncello, and catch the tender back to the Argonaut before its six-thirty departure. Sara and Damian endorsed her plan. Damian seemed pleased that he and Pastel would not be chaperoned. Before leaving Sara, Pastel said she would call on her cell phone if any problems arose. Sara commended her suggestion, but admitted having left her cell phone on the ship. Pastel couldn't believe anyone would be without their cell phone.

On her own now, Sara ambled along the by-ways of Pompeii, being careful not to trip on the uneven paving stones. She tried to recall places that she and David had found especially interesting. Bakeries and a brothel came to mind. She remembered the guide, an elderly Italian who had taught history in Naples. When he learned that the couple were newlyweds, he began discussing the Pompeiians' love of erotic art. One story he told involved a visit by King Francis of Naples and his wife and daughter to an exhibit of particularly provocative art. What they saw so embarrassed them that he ordered all the erotic art to be locked away. The former exhibit finally was made available again to the public in the nineteen sixties, but minors were only allowed to see it in the presence of a parent or guardian.

Sara repeatedly tried to envision David and her strolling among the ruins, the weather that day, and what they wore, but the only images she could conjure up were of Pompeiians desperately fleeing the approaching river of molten lava from Vesuvius. She flinched at the thought of people suddenly realizing they could not outrun the boiling flow and crouching behind stone walls to await death. So distressing were the scenes that formed in Sara's head that she found it difficult to continue sightseeing. The very air she breathed seemed heavy with dread and disappointment. She had come to Pompeii hoping to reconnect with fond memories of a treasured adventure with her husband only to be reminded of the ever-present threat of violent death. Once regarded as a gift, Sara's ability to form detailed mental images now seemed more of a curse.

After walking for over an hour. The terrible visions finally ceased. Sara began to picture life in Pompeii as it had been lived before the volcano erupted. Shop owners waiting on customers. Children frolicking in the streets. Bakers making bread in large, open-air ovens. Women tending their gardens. Men drinking in bars. People relaxing in public baths, praying to their gods, attending performances in the amphitheater, and swimming in the natatorium. Sara's mood brightened with these imaginings.

Before she knew it, the time had come to meet up with her friends. She hoped they had enjoyed being together. Coming to Pompeii with Damian, she understood, had been a big step for Pastel. She felt a mother's pride that the young woman overcame an obstacle.

After descending a long flight of steps at the site's far end, Sara walked back to where she was supposed to meet Damian and Pastel and sat on a bench. A passing tourist with a watch told her the time was a little after four o'clock. Crowds of exiting visitors began to parade past Sara. She kept looking for Pastel and Damian, but by four thirty they still had not shown up. The site soon would be closing. Sara began to worry that something bad had happened to her companions. She also fretted about possibly missing the Argonaut's departure. Had Damian somehow managed to get lost again? Or perhaps Pastel started chatting with someone and lost track of the time, as she had done in Meteora.

"It's a mother's fate to worry about others," Sara reminded herself. "I worried about Marie when she was young. I worried about my mother when she was old. I worried about David a lot, especially when he didn't come home from the university until late on the night of the Unite the Right rally in Charlottesville. Whenever he flew somewhere to meet donors, I worried that his plane might crash."

The longer she waited, the more upset Sara became. At first her upset was aimed at Damian and Pastel, but when she realized forgetting her cell phone was her fault, she grew angry at herself. Now she faced indecision about what to do. If there was one thing Sara the Practical hated above all others, it was uncertainty about what to do. Should she continue waiting? Should she contact the local police? Should she catch a taxi back to the ship? It might already be too late to get back in time. Sara was working herself into a frenzied state when she heard Pastel yelling her name.

Damian ran toward her, while Pastel waited at a distance. Sara noticed that she leaned on a cane. Damian explained that Pastel had been taking a photograph of him when a cluster of tourists in a hurry rushed past, causing her to take a hard fall onto the rocky walkway. She had no time to break the fall. Her right leg struck a sharp rock and began to bleed.

Fearing Pastel might have sustained a fracture, Damian located the nearest medical facility on his cell phone and drove Pastel to it. The attending physician doubted the leg was broken, just a bad sprain. He cleaned the wound and bandaged it, warning that the leg probably would swell and develop a large bruise. He recommended ibuprofen for pain.

Sara walked over to Pastel and gently hugged her. "We've got to get back to Sorrento," she exclaimed. "Once we're on the highway, we should contact someone on the ship and ask them to find out if the captain will delay the ship's departure."

"It's my fault we'll be late," Pastel said. "I'll call Dad."

Pastel was in obvious pain as she limped to the car. Once seated, she searched her backpack for the cell phone. "I don't believe this," she screamed. "I must have left my cell phone at the clinic. It's not in my backpack where I always keep it. Damian, we have to go back to the clinic. I'd be totally lost without my cell phone."

Sara asked how far away the medical facility was. Damian said it was a fifteen-minute drive. Sara suggested that Pastel use Damian's cell phone to call her father. After she tried unsuccessfully to reach him, Damian gave her the number of his parents. She noticed his cell phone battery was low.

Mr. Diaz answered and asked where they were. Pastel told him it was too long a story to recount. At the moment she needed him to find out if the captain would hold the ship until they returned to Sorrento. He agreed to check immediately and get back to her.

A few minutes later, just as they reached the clinic, Mr. Diaz called back. He explained that the captain would only delay embarkation for an excursion organized by the cruise line. Individuals who made their own arrangements for land trips had to secure transportation to the next port of call, in this case Civitavecchia outside of Rome. Driving there, Mr. Diaz added, would take around three to four hours via the A-1 highway. Before ending the call, Pastel requested that he notify her father of what happened.

Damian ran into the clinic to retrieve Pastel's cell phone. Sara found it hard to believe the young woman was in such a panic about leaving it. When Damian returned and handed the cell phone to her, she broke into tears of relief and made an effort to hug him, but the pain of twisting around to do so produced additional tears.

At this point Sara's penchant for practicality kicked into gear. Arrangements needed to be made. The car rental agency in Sorrento had to be contacted. Could the renters return the Toyota in Civitavecchia? Hotel accommodations had to be reserved for the evening. First and foremost, directions to the A-1 were required.

Pastel used her cell phone to get directions for the trip to Civitavecchia. Sara then requested the cell phone so she could call the car rental agency. Her request to return the car in Civitavecchia was approved, but for an exorbitant extra charge that Sara agreed to cover. Phone reception was spotty going through the coastal mountains near Naples so Sara decided to contact a hotel later.

Once on the A-1, traffic moved along at a fast clip. After almost an hour on the highway, Pastel received a call from Simone. She sounded distressed and asked to speak to Sara.

"I tried reaching you after the ship left Sorrento, but you weren't in your room or at the bar, and you didn't answer your cell phone. I contacted Damian's parents and found out you missed the boat. Will you still be able to go with me to Rome tomorrow?"

"Of course, Simone," Sara replied, trying to calm her. "We'll reach the port of Rome before you will. The three of us will find a place to spend the night and then board the ship after it docks. I believe the Argonaut is scheduled to arrive around seven in the morning. I'll need to shower and change my clothes and grab a bite to eat. Then we can head to Rome."

"That will be wonderful," Simone responded, sounding clearly relieved. "You're finding ways to be adventuresome after all, aren't you?" she added with a laugh.

Pastel overheard the conversation and asked if she could tag along with Sara and Simone. Rome was a place she longed to visit. Still on the phone, Simone said Pastel was welcome to accompany them. After the call ended, Sara explained that Simone wished to visit someone who had been special to her, but she hadn't a clue who that person might be.

A little while later Sara and Pastel asked Damian to stop at the next petrol station so they could use the restroom. Pastel was asked to locate a hotel in Civitavecchia where they could spend the night. Using her cell phone, she found a place with a respected brand name, and Sara handed her a credit card and instructed her to reserve two rooms.

Both women rushed from the car when Damian finally pulled into a petrol station. In the restroom, Pastel asked Sara if she could stay with her that night. Sara said she assumed that would be the arrangement and welcomed the company.

The three travelers reached Civitavecchia a little before nine o'clock and returned the Toyota. The clerk at the rental agency was getting ready to close for the night and offered to drive them to the hotel. After checking in, they grabbed appetizers and glasses of Chianti Classico at the hotel bar. Damian admitted being exhausted from all the driving and worrying about Pastel. He informed his companions that he planned to sleep as long as possible in the morning and would not be accompanying them to the ship. Sara and Pastel thanked him for being a good sport and hugged him.

After picking up ibuprofen for Pastel along with toothbrushes and toothpaste from the front desk, the weary travelers went to their rooms. Sara and Pastel took turns using the bathroom, then went to bed. Pastel said it felt good to take the weight off her leg and lie down.

"You know," Sara began, "I haven't slept with anyone since David died. That's almost three years ago."

"I've got you beat," Pastel responded. "It's been over four years for me."

"The other day you mentioned being mistreated by Jeremy and needing to seek the safety of a women's shelter. Do you mind my asking what happened?"

Pastel frowned and stared at the ceiling. "It's my own fault in a way," she admitted.

"There's never an excuse for abuse," Sara interrupted.

"That would have made a good slogan for the shelter. I blame myself to some extent because I knew Jeremy was interested in me mostly so he could gain access to my father. We were graduate students together, and he admired Dad. Told me he wanted to write his dissertation about him. Dad saw right through him. Called him a user and a loser."

"So, what happened?"

"When Dad decided to have nothing to do with the guy, Jeremy started taking it out on me. Verbally at first, then physically. I told him we were over and refused to see him. That's when he started stalking me. I withdrew from my doctoral program and moved to a new apartment, but he found out where I was and began leaving threatening notes. That's when I decided to enter the shelter. After hearing the stories of other residents, though, I realized my situation could have been a lot worse."

Sara reached across the bed and held Pastel's hand. "No one deserves what you experienced." She turned off the bedside lamp. Darkness brought silence, then another question from Sara.

"What do you think about Damian?"

"You're asking if I think we have a future together? Perhaps as friends, but nothing more."

"How come?"

"Because I don't think he'd push me enough. Damian is all about becoming a well-known scholar. If we were a couple, I'm certain he would accept me just as I am."

"That's a bad thing?" Sara asked.

"I know, it sounds crazy, but I need someone who'll push me beyond my comfort zone, like you and Simone did when you got me to enter the writing contest."

Nothing more was said. Pastel quickly fell asleep, but Sara lay awake and wondered whether David could have pushed her more when she decided to discontinue her art studies.

CHAPTER 11

WEDNESDAY, SEPTEMBER 21, 2022

When the Argonaut docked at the port of Civitavecchia, Sara and Pastel were waiting near the passport control portal to board. Pastel continued using her cane to steady herself, but she felt the pain was less intense than the previous day. Prior to the ship's arrival, Sara made arrangements for a car and driver to take the three women to Rome at nine-thirty that morning. The trip would take about an hour and a half, depending on traffic.

When the gangplank was secured, Sara and Pastel were permitted to board before passengers on the ship disembarked. They rushed to their rooms to shower and change clothes. Sara checked in with Simone, who was relieved to learn her companions had arrived safely. They agreed to meet in the departure lounge in an hour. When Sara spotted the framed photograph of David, it dawned on her that she had been too busy lately to think much about him. A silent, sad apology was offered. As she showered, Sara acknowledged that the cruise so far had not brought the closure she sought for her relationship with David and the married phase of her life. She had trouble, in fact, articulating exactly what the cruise's impact on her thus far had been.

Pastel and Sara unexpectedly ran into each other at the barista bar. They laughed at their still moist hair. Both ordered lattes and Danish pastry. Sara had changed into a sleeveless blue dress and flats. Pastel wore a short, pleated skirt and snug tank top along with sandals. They reassured each other that there was no rain in the forecast.

Simone was chatting with the concierge when Sara and Pastel arrived at the departure lounge. They simultaneously complimented Simone on her multi-colored dashiki. Sara sensed that Simone was nervous about the upcoming journey to Rome, but when she inquired, Simone nonchalantly replied that getting off the ship would be a relief. Then she asked about Pastel's cane and learned that she had been jostled by a tour group at Pompeii. Simone wondered if Pastel wouldn't be better off resting her sore leg, but her young friend said nothing was going to prevent her from seeing one of the world's most beautiful cities.

After leaving the Argonaut, the women searched for their driver. Filing past a gauntlet of vendors hawking various tours, Pastel spotted a short, gray-haired man holding a sign that read "Castle party." He introduced himself as Gabriele and guided his passengers to a black Mercedes sedan.

When everyone was seated and buckled in, Gabriele asked Sara where in Rome she wished to go. Sara turned to Simone, who responded. "We need to drive to the Esquilino district, near the Termini Train Station. The apartment is just off Viale Manzoni."

"This is not the most beautiful part of Rome," Gabriele replied.

"I am no longer as beautiful as I once was," Simone responded, "but my friends don't complain."

"Many immigrants in this part of Rome," he added.

"And I want to visit one of them," Simone declared authoritatively.

When they reached the highway, Gabriele commented that traffic didn't look very heavy for a Wednesday. "Maybe some people stay home because it might rain."

Sara and Pastel just looked at each other and grimaced.

"Can you tell us about the person you wish to visit?" Sara asked Simone.

"His name is Amadou Mbaye. We were students together at the Sorbonne in Paris. I was on a one-year fellowship as part of my doctoral program. We spent a great deal of time together discussing our research interests and traveling around Europe. When I returned to Missouri to work on my dissertation, we communicated for a while, but then I lost track of him. Actually, I was led to believe he had died."

"What happened?" Pastel asked.

"I don't really know. When I tried to find out why Amadou stopped replying to my letters, a mutual friend in Paris wrote that Amadou had returned to Senegal to see his family and suffered a serious accident. Amadou's adviser at the Sorbonne contacted his sister and learned that the injuries were life threatening. That's all I could find out. I didn't know where in Senegal he was, and I had no contact information.

"How'd you discover he was still alive?" Sara asked.

"Sheer serendipity. When I sold my house, I started packing up my academic books so I could donate them. Many of the books were sent to me as complimentary copies from publishers. I usually stick them on a shelf and forget about them. One of these books I happened to glance at as I was packing it. The book contained a collection of short stories by émigré African writers."

"Don't tell me Amadou contributed a story," Sara said excitedly.

"That he did. It was a bittersweet tale of an aging fado singer in Portugal. If you know about the Portuguese term, saudade, that's what the story is all about."

Sara and Pastel exchanged puzzled looks.

"Saudade refers to a deep emotional state of longing for someone who is absent," Simone explained.

"Like melancholy?" Pastel asked.

"Like melancholy on steroids."

Gabriele overheard the conversation and commented, "We have similar words in Italian. It is malinconico, to wish for something with little hope of getting it."

The impact of the discussion caught Sara by surprise. She had spent almost three years stricken by longing for David, yet knowing he would never return. Now she wondered if those feelings were losing their intensity.

Simone immediately sensed what Sara was thinking. "I'm sorry for bringing up the subject, Sara. My guess is you're well aware of saudade."

Sara did not respond, but she couldn't help wondering if the loss of longing was a blessing or an emotional deficit. Pastel asked Simone to continue with her story.

"I checked the publication date for the short story collection. It was 2020. I realized, of course, Amadou might have written the story years earlier, but I also knew he hadn't written it when we both were in Paris. I contacted the publisher and found out Amadou was on the faculty of the American University of Rome. When I emailed a colleague I knew at the university, he replied that Amadou retired when the Pandemic hit Italy. He sent me the address listed for Amadou in the 2020 faculty register, but he didn't know if Amadou still lived there."

"Did you try contacting Amadou?" Pastel asked.

"I did not. Don't ask me why. I certainly could have. The cruise already was booked, so I made up my mind to go to the address when the ship reached the port of Rome. If it turns out Amadou has moved elsewhere, so be it. We weren't meant to reconnect."

Sara took note of the casual way Simone spoke of possibly not making contact with Amadou, but she wasn't convinced. While her friend, in many ways, was an enigma to Sara, she was willing to wager that Simone and Amadou had been lovers and that seeing him again, especially given her illness, meant a great deal to her.

Upon reaching the central part of Rome, the women asked Gabriele to point out any landmarks. Sara was struck by the chaotic traffic and how every driver relied on their horn as much as their accelerator to negotiate the busy streets and avenues. After passing the enormous central train station and making several turns, Gabriele suddenly jammed on his brakes, nearly depositing Pastel in the front seat. Pulling over to the curb, he pointed to a nondescript apartment building and repeated the address Simone had given him.

Pastel got out of the Mercedes and tried to assist Simone, but she still was unsteady because of her bruised leg. Sara offered to help Simone after she paid Gabriele. The driver asked if they desired a ride back to the ship, but she told him they would catch a taxi. He warned her to agree on the charge with the driver before climbing into the vehicle.

Amadou's apartment was located on the third floor. Fortunately for Simone and Pastel, the building had an elevator, but the squeaky relic was barely big enough to hold the three women. Simone appeared to be lost in thought, so much so that Pastel had to grab her by the elbow and usher her out of the elevator before the door closed on her. When they reached the apartment door, Simone hesitated.

"What if he's married?" Simone asked.

"You didn't find that out earlier?' Sara stammered.

"I guess I didn't want to know," Simone whispered.

When Simone made no move to knock on the door, Sara did so.

"What if no one is home?" Pastel asked.

Just then Sara heard a voice inside calling out in French. Simone responded in French. The door slowly opened, and a short woman wearing a burka and a green head scarf with gold trim peeked out.

"Bon jour," Simone said with a smile. She proceeded to speak to the woman in French. Sara picked up a word here and there, but failed to catch the drift of the conversation. All of a sudden, Simone stepped toward the woman and embraced her. When Simone turned around, she was in tears.

The woman gestured for the visitors to enter. As they did, Simone wiped her eyes and explained that their host was Madina Mbeya, Amadou's younger sister.

"Has something happened to Amadou?" Sara inquired.

Simone looked away. "The gods apparently relish irony. He passed away three months ago from COVID, around the same time I found out my cancer was inoperable."

First Sara, then Pastel hugged Simone. They, too, had tears in their eyes.

Medina motioned for her guests to be seated in the small, but comfortable living room, and then excused herself. Simone indicated she was going to make tea.

"I had a premonition that my Amadou was no longer of this world," Simone quietly noted. "That he was still alive after all these years was just too good to be true. I'm one of those star-crossed persons fated to be alone."

"Do you think Amadou wrote the short story for you?" Pastel asked.

Simone gave Pastel a knowing look, but did not answer her question. "I'm sorry that Medina doesn't speak English," she said. "We don't have to stay here very long, but I need to learn more about Amadou's life before we leave."

"Take as long as you want," Sara insisted. "We can wait down-stairs if you'd prefer."

"Not at all. Medina would be offended if we didn't stay for tea."

While Sara and Pastel enjoyed the tea and biscuits, Simone followed Medina into another room. They returned fifteen minutes later. Simone's eyes had reddened considerably. As Medina poured more tea, Simone explained that she was shown Amadou's tiny office. It was barely big enough for a desk, a chair, and a bookshelf. Medina said she hadn't touched anything since Amadou's death. On his desk was a framed photograph of Simone and Amadou in Lisbon. When she shared this discovery, Simone broke down and cried.

After their second cup of tea, the visitors asked if they could use the restroom. Pastel and Sara stopped at Amadou's office to see the photograph. Once they all were done, the visitors hugged their host. Medina asked Simone if she wanted anything from Amadou's office, but she declined the offer, saying that her memories were more than sufficient reminders of a beautiful relationship.

The three women left the apartment building, and Simone suggested they find a nearby café and enjoy a light lunch. She promised to apprise her companions of what she learned from Medina. A five-minute walk brought them to an inviting trattoria with a small patio. They chose a table near the café's front door. In a few minutes an aproned middle-aged woman greeted them in Italian. Simone asked if she spoke English, and she indicated with her fingers that she knew a little bit. Simone tried French with more success. She requested menus and bottled water for everyone.

"When Medina first came to the door," Simone began, "I thought she was Amadou's wife."

"That must have been a heartbreaker," Sara stated.

"Not as heartbreaking as finding out he recently died from COVID. Just think, had there been no Pandemic, we would have been reunited after forty years. So many lives have been lost or disrupted because of the virus." Simone grew quiet.

"Did you ever find out what happened to Amadou when he went back to Senegal?" Pastel inquired.

"That's another lamentable tale."

The server returned with menus and bottled water.

"Amadou went back to Dakar after Ramadan to see his family. While he was there, he borrowed a bicycle in order to visit the national library for an essay he was researching. A motorist struck him, and he was knocked unconscious. He regained consciousness in the hospital and learned that his right leg was severely injured and needed to be amputated before infection spread. As a result of the amputation, ironically, he contracted sepsis and nearly died. It took more than a year for Amadou to recover fully and learn to walk with a prosthetic leg."

"What about your efforts to contact him?" Sara asked.

"He found out that I had communicated with his friend in Paris. According to Medina, he loved me but felt he could never be the kind of husband that I deserved. He instructed his friend to contact me and say that he was unlikely to survive. At the time I seriously considered flying to Senegal, but the friend advised me not to. I was in the midst of completing my dissertation, so I focused on that in the hopes that Amadou would contact me if, by some miracle, he survived."

"Would you have minded being with Amadou, had you known what happened to him?" Pastel asked.

"What do you think? I didn't fall in love with Amadou because he had two good legs. I fell in love with the person he was. It grieves me beyond words to know we could have been together all this time if only I had followed my heart and flown to Senegal."

"Sounds like Amadou was the great love of your life," Sara replied.

"I never once considered anyone else," Simone declared with the fervor of a Baptist preacher. "True desire is all-consuming. I once tried to write about it, but I struggled to find the appropriate words. Sara, you have a vivid imagination. I thought I did as well, but I couldn't even imagine living with any other man after falling in love with Amadou. That's what I mean by true desire. There actually was a time when I considered suicide. Only by focusing all of my energy on my career and my students was I able to move past those dark days."

Hearing Simone's confession, Sara felt profound sadness for her friend and a touch of sadness for herself as well, though she couldn't explain why.

She didn't say anything, but Pastel appeared to be taking in what she was hearing. When Simone asked if something she said had upset her, Pastel responded, "You've given me a lot to reflect on. I know about your ex-husband, his drug issues, and how he abused you. What I don't understand is how you were able to form a strong attachment for Amadou after such an awful experience with a man?"

The server returned and asked if the women were ready to order. Simone shook her head and said they needed a little more time.

"Just because my husband was an insecure addict who felt threatened by my success doesn't mean that other men would have felt the same way. Wouldn't it be foolish to generalize based on a sample of one?"

Pastel smiled. "I know it's not rational, but I'm still fearful around men."

"How's that for irony? Sara noted. "You're afraid of being with men, and I'm afraid of being alone. I think we need some wine."

"I understand you weren't afraid of Damian when you went to Pompeii," Simone observed.

Pastel turned toward Sara. "We had a chaperone. Besides, I knew there was no future for me with Damian."

Simone felt several drops of rain just as the server re-appeared and suggested the women move indoors. Once in the cozy trattoria, they ordered several pasta dishes to share and a bottle of pinot grigio.

"I know you booked the cruise before finding out that Amadou was living in Rome," Sara stated. "So why did you decide to go on a cruise when you knew how sick you were?"

"Was I supposed to spend the last days of my life watching television and wallowing in self-pity?"

"Okay, I get that you wanted to travel while you were still able to do so, but I would have thought Paris might have been your preferred destination."

"I never had been on a cruise before, and I liked the fact you could see many places without packing and unpacking a lot. I chose the Argonaut because its final destination was Lisbon. That's where Amadou and I fell in love."

The rainy weather prompted Sara to share a story. "David and I visited Rome on our honeymoon," she began. "I desperately wanted to see Michelangelo's masterpiece, the Sistine Chapel, but David was a history buff and preferred to visit the Forum and Pantheon.

As usual, he got his way. I still can picture us standing in the Forum ruins with no umbrellas or raincoats getting soaked to the bone by a torrential downpour."

"Did you refuse to speak to him for the rest of the honeymoon?" Pastel asked.

"I wouldn't have done that," Sara responded, "but I did insist on choosing the sites we'd see in Florence. Getting wet was well worth it."

"I don't want to sound like I'm bragging, but Amadou and I never disagreed on where to go or what to do."

"If only my parents enjoyed the same compatibility," Pastel commented.

Simone looked at Sara. "Why didn't you tell me about wanting to see the Sistine Chapel? Do you think we have time to go now? Vatican City is pretty close."

"That would have been nice, but we don't have tickets. I don't want you to stand in line in the rain while we wait to purchase tickets. Checking on Amadou was much more important. Besides, my dream of becoming an artist, like much of Rome, is ancient history. It's not that important anymore."

The server returned with the pasta dishes. Her young assistant opened the wine, gave Sara the cork to sniff, and filled three glasses.

"If I may ask," Simone began, "what is important to you now?"

"That's what I'm trying to figure out. At the moment, I guess what's important is enjoying this wine and pasta."

After a harrowing taxi ride by a driver who looked all of fifteen years of age, Sara, Simone, and Pastel arrived at the dock and boarded the Argonaut. Simone thanked her friends for accompanying her and apologized again for Sara not seeing the Sistine Chapel. Pastel went to check on her father, Simone sought the comfort of her bed, and Sara decided to visit Gyorgy and try his Man Overboard cocktail. She also planned on figuring out how to spend the next day in Florence.

The delighted expression on Gyorgy's face when Sara arrived pleased her greatly. When she admitted being ready to try the Man Overboard drink, he asked to see her driver's license to make sure she was old enough.

"You're not fooling me, Gyorgy. You want to see my driver's license so you can get my address."

"To order Man Overboard, one must be at least fifty years old," he deadpanned.

"Guess I can't order one. How about a glass of chocolate milk?"

"I will make a special exception for you. Man Overboard coming up."

Sara watched Gyorgy closely to see what ingredients went into a Man Overboard. She saw him pour bourbon and a little yellow Chartreuse into a shaker, but then he walked away. Whatever he added after that remained a mystery. He returned with the cocktail in a chilled martini glass and advised Sara to sip slowly.

Whatever the concoction was, Sara found it to be delicious. She detected hints of cherry and lemon along with flavors she had trouble identifying. When she pleaded for Gyorgy to divulge the secret ingredients, all he said was "dragon fruit."

A few minutes later Pastel showed up and asked about Sara's plans for Livorno.

"I thought about taking the train to Florence."

"Would you like some company?"

"Normally I'd love it, but tomorrow I just need some time with David."

"Do you mean Michelangelo's David or your David?"

"Both of them."

"I understand. Anyway, I wanted to let you know that my father wants to treat the three amigas to dinner tomorrow night at La Boheme. He made reservations for eight o'clock."

"That sounds lovely, Pastel. After being on my own all day, company for dinner will be most welcome."

Pastel departed and Sara continued enjoying her Man Overboard as she jotted down several places in Florence she wanted to visit. The list included the Uffizi Gallery, the Accademia Gallery, a stroll across the Ponte Vecchio, and the Boboli Gardens. As she tried to estimate the time required to cover all four destinations, Trevor appeared and noted that Sara's drink was almost finished.

"Can I buy you another of whatever you're having?" he asked.

"If you do, Gyorgy will have to rename his signature drink Woman Overboard. It's a potent potion. Will you be going to Florence tomorrow?"

"To be honest, I don't think I'm quite ready for that," he replied. "Florence was a very special place for Ava and me. Going there would remind me of the times when our relationship was magical."

Sara fought the urge to ask what Trevor meant by "magical." He went on to say his plan was to take a taxi to Pisa.

"As an architect, I'm fascinated by the measures that have been taken to keep the Leaning Tower from falling."

The two went on chatting for an hour. Sara had a glass of wine and shared her experience with Simone and Pastel in Rome. Trevor tried a Man Overboard and recounted his visit to St. Peter's Cathedral and the Sistine Chapel. Sara was relieved to hear that he had to wait in line for over an hour before getting to see the magnificent chapel. Skipping a trip to the Vatican had been the right decision for her.

Sitting at the bar carrying on a pleasant conversation with an attractive man triggered a long dormant feeling in Sara. More of an urge than a specific yearning. Intriguing to be sure, but also slightly dangerous. Certainly not a feeling she was willing to discuss or examine more carefully. Sara attributed it to her Man Overboard.

Later that evening when Sara returned to her room, she considered what Trevor had said about Florence and wondered if there was any place that she and David visited that might now be too painful for her to see again. It bothered her that no such place came readily to mind.

CHAPTER 12

THURSDAY, SEPTEMBER 22, 2022

Sara slept fitfully thanks to persistent night sweats that compelled her to get up every hour or so to dry off. When she finally drifted off into what seemed like sleep, her cell phone buzzed. The bedside clock read five thirty-five. Praying that something terrible hadn't happened to Marie and Marcus, she answered the call.

"Morning, Mom. Sorry to get you up so early."

"Randy, is that you? Are you okay? You weren't in an accident, were you?" There was no concealing the panic in her voice.

"Nothing bad has happened, but something good has."

Sara took a deep breath. Had her love'em-and-leave'em son finally met someone he wanted to marry? Why else would he call her in the middle of a European cruise?

"I bid for temporary duty out of Dulles International Airport and just heard I got approved for a month, starting now. So, I checked on your itinerary with Marie. It looks like I'll have a layover in Barcelona the day after tomorrow, when you're there. How'd you like to get together?"

"Oh! Randy. I'm thrilled. What a special surprise. It's been too long. Will you come to the ship?"

"We're scheduled to arrive several hours after you reach port. Why don't we plan to meet for lunch at El Quatre Gats in the old section of town. I've heard the atmosphere there is right up your alley. Artsy."

"That sounds perfect. Does noon work for you?"

"Unless we're delayed by weather, which looks unlikely right now. Noon should be fine. Just bring your cell phone in case I need to reach you."

"I can't wait. I love you, Randy."

"I love you, too, Mom. Now go back to sleep."

Sara, of course, could no more go back to sleep than she could swim the English Channel. She had not seen Randy since the Pandemic began. In the shower, she decided to invite Pastel to join her. Pastel and Randy were close in age. Who knows? They might hit it off.

By the time Sara arrived at the breakfast buffet, the Argonaut was docking at Livorno. Not knowing when or even if she'd get lunch, Sara decided to eat a hearty breakfast of eggs and pancakes, fruit, and lots of coffee. Florence was a city best visited on foot. Burning off her breakfast calories would not be a problem.

No sooner had she finished eating than the cruise director announced that disembarkation could begin. After a speedy return to her room for sunscreen, the UVA baseball cap that David gave her when Virginia won the national championship, and a light jacket, Sara left the ship and asked for directions to the train station. A brief taxi ride brought her to the station, just in time to watch the train to Florence depart.

A young man in a military uniform noticed the crestfallen look on Sara's face and explained that another train to Florence would arrive soon. Forty-two trains a day, he said, made the hour and a half trip. A half hour later, Sara and the young man boarded the next train. It was crowded with people, most of whom were masked. Before donning her mask, Sara thanked the man for helping her. As it turned out, only one pair of seats was unoccupied. The man, who introduced himself as Enrico, asked if Sara minded him sitting with her. She welcomed the company of the polite young man because he spoke good English and bore a striking resemblance to her son.

As the train pulled out of the station, Sara asked Enrico his reason for traveling to Florence. He explained that his aunt passed away the previous week, and his commanding officer gave him permission to attend her funeral. The young man obviously loved his aunt a great deal. He had lived with her for a time when his life was not going so well.

Eventually there was a lull in the conversation. Sara noticed how noisy the passenger car had become. Several rows ahead, two men sitting across the aisle from each other were yelling in Italian. The older of the two suddenly stood up and made a threatening gesture toward the younger man. Enrico quickly jumped up and rushed forward, speaking in Italian. The older man reluctantly sat down. Passengers started clapping for Enrico and thanking him for intervening.

When he returned to his seat, Enrico explained that all of Italy was on edge these days. The two men had been arguing about the government. The Prime Minister resigned in July, and national elections were scheduled for September 25. Sara admitted not following the news during her cruise. Enrico was of the opinion that the new government probably would involve some kind of coalition, most likely centrist party members and right-wingers. Sara gathered there was great concern in Italy, as in her own country, over the large number of undocumented immigrants arriving every day.

"You know," Sara said with a motherly smile, "that was a very brave thing you did, preventing those men from getting into a fight."

"I am deeply saddened," Enrico began, "by how divided my country has become. Religion once united us, but that no longer is true. I believe your country has similar problems."

Sara nodded in agreement and said that Americans Enrico's age was disillusioned with politics.

"The only way to avoid being disillusioned," Enrico replied, "is to have no illusions in the first place."

"You are wise for your age," Sara said with a smile. She went on to say that America lacked inspiring young leaders like John F. Kennedy and Barack Obama. "Now we have a gerontocracy. Next year we'll most likely face a choice between two old men who represent the past, not the future."

Time passed very quickly. Before Sara knew it, the conductor announced their arrival in Florence. She thanked Enrico for being such good company and expressed her hope that his aunt's funeral would provide an opportunity to reconnect with family members. After parting, she couldn't help recalling her trauma over David's funeral. Still in shock, she was unable to deliver a eulogy. Marie and Randy, however, rose to the occasion and delivered heartfelt remarks about their father.

At the train station's information desk, Sara asked how far it was to the Galleria dell'Accademia. The clerk said she could walk there in five minutes and marked the route on a small city map. As she joined the parade of tourists leaving Santa Maria Novella Station, Sara tried to remember details from her former visit to Florence with David.

She recalled arriving in Florence in the evening and feeling a chill in the air. David had booked an inexpensive hotel near Ponte Vecchio. All the museums were closed for the day, so they checked into the hotel and took a leisurely stroll around central Florence. They must have found someplace to eat dinner, but Sara had no recollection of where they dined or what they ate. She recalled holding hands with David during the walk, which was unusual because he tended to walk at a faster pace. Sara used to joke with her friends that David preferred her to follow behind him like a stereotypical Asian wife in old movies.

The imposing façade of the Galleria dell'Accademia soon came into view. Sara purchased a ticket, which had soared in price since her previous visit. She didn't plan to stay very long. The art at the Uffizi was of greater interest to her, but she longed to once again admire Michelangelo's statue of David. Locating the statue wasn't difficult. Just follow the crowd.

Sara regretted not having the statue all to herself, but at least it towered over the onlookers in the Galleria's rotunda. When she visited with her own David, the crowd was much smaller, though the reactions were similar. Men commented on how well-endowed young David was, while women silently stared and fantasized, their mouths agape. This time Sara overheard an English-speaking guide pointing out that Michelangelo's David was not circumcised, though most men in David's time were.

After circling the crowd, Sara found an unoccupied alcove that allowed her to appreciate the exquisiteness of the sculpture, from David's finely carved hands and legs to the placid expression on his face. The more she studied the statue, the more captivated she became. How could Michelangelo have brought life to stone? Such pristine beauty, so erotic in its perfection. Sara shuddered as a frisson passed across her loins. Tears formed in her eyes, a reaction to beauty that Sara used to experience frequently. David as a rule was less emotional. Only three times had she ever seen him moved to tears: when Randy and Marie were born and when Barack Obama was elected President.

As Sara left the rotunda, she overheard a tourist ask her companion, "Do you think human beings were meant to look so perfect?" Reflecting on the woman's query, Sara decided that it was individuals' imperfections that made them fascinating. Best to leave perfection to the gods.

According to Sara's map, the Uffizi Galleria was roughly five kilometers from the Galleria dell'Accademia. After a brisk walk, Sara sensed her destination must be nearby because she spotted a line of people sneaking around a large building, waiting to purchase tickets. It took her half an hour to gain access to the exhibits. Sara, of course, understood the impossibility of seeing all the Uffizi had to offer in the few hours she had available. After consulting the museum's brochure, she decided first to visit Botticelli's magnificent "Birth of Venus" and "Spring." The self-portrait of Elisabeth Le Brun would be saved for last.

At the "Birth of Venus," the crowd made it impossible to get close enough to study technical aspects of Botticelli's artwork. Decades had passed since Sara applied the analytical skills she acquired in her college art classes, but she still recalled how to examine composition, brush technique, and use of light and color. When she moved on to the painter's charming embodiment of spring, only a few visitors were present. Sara took advantage of the opportunity to conduct a close-up assessment of Botticelli's style.

Satisfied with her viewing of "Spring," Sara moved on to Le Brun's self-portrait. No sooner did she locate the painting than a flood of memories washed over her. She vividly recalled how David excused himself in order to wander around the piazza in search of a decent Sangiovese. Though he claimed to value great art, Sara felt he said such things simply to please her.

The first time Sara saw the self-portrait, she could have been viewing her own image. Le Brun looked straight ahead at the onlooker, a daring pose for a female artist at the time. A straw hat perched atop the curls that framed her beguiling face. More than one fellow viewer commented to Sara on how much she resembled the renowned French portrait painter.

In the presence of Le Brun's self-portrait almost three decades earlier, Sara had felt unexpectedly hopeful that she, too, still had enough time to pursue her love of art in a serious way. David's need to launch his own career might require a slight delay in pursuing her goal, but there was no reason at the time to think a career in art was beyond her grasp. If going to Paris on an art fellowship was unrealistic, a graduate-level art program closer to home surely could be found.

Both David and Sara wanted children, and Sara believed she could manage family responsibilities as well as develop her artistic skills. After all, hadn't Elisabeth Le Brun given birth to a daughter when she was twenty-five? Not even divorce and the chaos of the French Revolution prevented her from achieving acclaim in the art world. When she no longer was welcome in France, the intrepid artist traveled to the courts of Europe painting monarchs and other nobility.

The longer Sara stood gazing at Le Brun's self-portrait and conjuring up memories, the more melancholy she became. Taking a seat on a nearby bench, she permitted sadness to envelop her. Why had she lost touch with her dreams? Sadness slowly morphed into anger. Not anger at David. He had a right to his own dreams. She'd never begrudge him that. Sara's anger was aimed at herself for not pushing to complete her training.

Despite her morose mood, Sara managed to experience an epiphany of sorts as she stared back at Le Brun. Her college instructors always tried to focus her attention on an artist's technique: the way they arranged their subject matter on canvas, the tools and materials they chose to convey an idea, how they managed to attract the viewer's attention. Now Sara realized that it was just as important to understand the artist as a person. How did she handle raising a child? What was her reaction to criticism? Did she confront physical challenges as she grew older? Sara wondered if she might have persisted in achieving her dream had she known more about Le Brun's life outside of art.

When she finally checked the time, Sara was amazed to discover she'd been sitting in front of Le Brun's self-portrait for over an hour. In order to reach the Argonaut before it departed Livorno, she needed to catch the four o'clock train. There was not enough time to eat lunch and also visit the Boboli Gardens. Despite consuming a hearty breakfast, Sara's stomach was growling. She decided to stroll across the Ponte Vecchio and find a vendor selling food to go.

The famous bridge crossing the Arno was packed with tourists, most of whom were unmasked. Sara figured the individuals wearing masks must have been local residents. After squeezing past two tour groups of slow-moving senior citizens, Sara spotted a vendor advertising calzones. She laughed because he looked like Chef Boyardee. The vendor had heard from other tourists that he resembled the chef on all those cans of American versions of Italian food, but he insisted the calzones he sold could never be sold in cans. Sara ordered one with cheese and sausage. Seating on the bridge was scarce, so she reversed course and found a bench on the shore.

Munching her calzones, Sara's thoughts turned to Enrico and his aunt's funeral? She wondered if he offered some words of remembrance. Her own failure to do so at David's funeral still bothered her and gave her yet another reason to be upset at herself. Before she knew it, Sara was feeling angry at herself for feeling angry at herself. She hadn't expected the second honeymoon cruise to generate such uncomfortable feelings of anger and guilt.

On the train back to Livorno, Sara chose to sit alone. That turned out to be a mistake. If she had found someone with whom to sit and chat, she might not have allowed herself to be consumed with disappointment. Enrico had been right. Those who become disillusioned have only themselves to blame for having illusions in the first place. Why would she ever expect a solo second honeymoon to produce only wonderful memories as well as bring closure to thirty years of marriage?

So preoccupied was Sara with her naivete and unrealistic expectations that she completely forgot about that night's dinner with Brendan Greene. Had she not run into Simone when she reboarded the ship, Sara might have spent the evening seeking solace with Gyorgy at the bar. Simone asked what Sara planned to wear to dinner, which seemed a little out of character. She impressed Sara as a person who made up her own mind on everything, including her wardrobe.

Sara was in no mood at that moment to think about what to wear, but she sensed that Simone considered dinner with Brendan Greene to be an important occasion. La Boheme was Argonaut's fanciest restaurant and the only one that required an additional charge. A high-necked, sleeveless black sheath was the only one of Sara's dresses that seemed appropriate. She also planned to bring a light sweater in case the air conditioning was too cool. Simone thanked Sara for her input and ambled back to her room.

After showering and drying her hair, Sara got dressed. Her mood brightened when she slipped into the black dress and added the jade necklace David brought her from China. After admiring herself in the full-length mirror, she decided to drop by Simone's room to see if her friend needed help zipping up her dress or desired an opinion about her choice of evening wear.

Simone greeted Sara in a dark green skirt and off-white, three-quarter sleeve blouse. Sara complimented her on the combination, but it was all too obvious her friend had lost a lot of weight since she purchased the items.

"I didn't expect to dress up when I packed for the cruise," Simone offered by way of apology. "I'd better eat a big dinner so I can fill out these clothes better."

By the time Sara and Simone arrived at La Boheme, Brendan and Pastel were seated and sharing a bottle of Sancerre. "Thank you for joining us," Brendan said as he slowly stood to greet his guests. "I've been wanting to show my appreciation for all the attention you've given my daughter."

"I can assure you," Simone replied, "the pleasure has been entirely ours. You have a remarkable daughter, worldly-wise beyond her years."

"Don't I know it," Brendan asserted. "Of course, you're aware I'm a writer, and I believe you also know Pastel's mother is an artist. It therefore goes without saying that neither of us is ever fully satisfied with anything we create." He paused briefly for effect. "With the sole exception being Pastel."

Pastel blushed.

"Do you think the two of you will ever get back together?" Sara asked.

Pastel turned and looked at her father.

"I'm afraid that would be unwise. We disagree on virtually everything. Where to live. With whom to associate. What to eat for breakfast. What events to attend. You name it. The one thing both of us agreed on was that Pastel should not become a writer."

"Why was that?" Simone inquired.

"As I've already made clear, neither of us is ever satisfied with our work. It's an artistic curse. A life of perpetual dissatisfaction is hardly a proper life, is it? We wanted Pastel to be happy and fulfilled."

"So, the two of you actually agreed on something else," Simone added.

"Help me understand," Sara began. "If writing is so unpleasant, why do you write?"

A wry smile formed on Brendan's lips. "You probably think I live to write, but that is not the case. In truth, I write to live, to keep from going mad."

"Can we change the subject?" Pastel interjected in a perturbed voice. "Would you like to try our Sancerre or have something else?"

"Sancerre is sauvignon blanc, isn't it?" Sara asked.

"You know your wine," Brendan replied.

"David was a wine geek. He always insisted that life is too short to drink lousy wine. Little did he know."

Simone ordered her usual Manhattan, straight up. Sara tried the Sancerre.

Brendan began firing questions at Sara and Simone. Where did they grow up? What were their youthful interests? Where had they traveled? Each time one of them answered, Brendan appropriated the response in order to talk about himself: where he grew up, what his youthful interests were, where he had traveled. Visibly upset by her father's behavior, Pastel apologized to Sara and Simone.

"I'm so sorry. My father asks a lot of questions so that he can reveal aspects of his own life."

Brendan did not appear bothered by his daughter's comment. Instead, he raised his wine glass. "A toast, my friends. How refreshing it is to hear the youthful voice of truth in this era of old men's lies."

Sara and Pastel clinked glasses with Brendan. Still waiting for her Manhattan, Simone raised her water glass in agreement.

"Allow me to try again," Brendan began as Pastel rolled her eyes. "I shall make a statement rather than ask a question. Simone, I've been reading on the Internet about your work. Your analysis of Richard Wright's writing is insightful and even courageous."

Her surprise evident, Simone asked, "Why courageous?"

"Because you were willing to state that Wright forfeited any credibility he might have had to speak for American blacks when he abandoned New York City and moved to Paris after the war."

"Compliment accepted," Simone said as she received her Manhattan. "Much of my academic career has focused on African American writers who left their native country. Many tried to continue speaking for their brothers and sisters back home, but no one, including James Baldwin, managed to do so authoritatively."

"I also found your discussion of racism in France to be very enlightening," Brendan added.

"Once again, thank you. Racism certainly exists in France, but it can be more subtle than in the U.S." Simone seemed pleased that Brendan took the time to explore her work.

The waiter arrived and distributed menus the size of atlases, then took five minutes describing in detail each of the specials. As the diners surveyed their many choices, Simone addressed Brendan regarding his own work.

"I've been examining some of your writings as well. In 'A Dangerous Peace,' you wrote that the focus of desire may shift, but desire itself can never be satisfied. I found this statement enigmatic."

"You had to dig pretty deep to find that one," Brendan replied with a grin. "Boris, if you recall, had a burning desire to be wise. The problem is that wisdom is cumulative and forever evolving. It's not a matter of compiling a certain amount of knowledge and then declaring that one is wise. Poor Boris didn't realize that what he desired ultimately was unattainable."

The conversation clearly intrigued Sara. "What if you have a burning desire to have a burning desire?" she asked.

"You make a very interesting point, Sara," Brendan responded. "If what you desire is desire itself, then I suppose it's possible to argue that such a desire can be satisfied."

"You've written a lot about men like Boris," Simone stated. "Men who don't get what they want. Often these individuals take out their frustrations through violence. What about women who don't get what they want?"

"I have never professed to understand the female psyche," Brendan said with a mouthful of amuse bouche. "My guess is that some women also resort to violence, if not physical violence, then psychological violence. Others, perhaps, simply choose to desire something different when they don't get what they want."

Having finished the Sancerre, Brendan requested a grenache from the sommelier.

"Pastel told us you're thinking about a new book," Sara commented. "Can you tell us something about it?"

Brendan feigned a frown. "You do know it's bad luck for a writer to disclose a new project, don't you?"

Sara apologized.

"But since you were interested enough to ask, I can tell you this. The main character is a man who believes in preemptive atonement."

Sara looked puzzled.

"In other words, he knows he is going to sin, so he atones in advance by undertaking small acts of kindness and generosity."

"How do you really know he's atoning in advance?" Simone asked. "If he's a chronic sinner, as you suggest, it would be hard to determine whether he's atoning for a past sin or a sin yet to be committed."

Brendan became absorbed for a moment with Simone's observation. "An excellent point," he finally stated. "There's a reason you're a professor and I'm just a writer."

The conversation continued to ebb and flow, depending on when food arrived and more drinks were served. Sara marveled at the broad range of topics that were covered, from the self-esteem of black men to contemporary trends in art to the sad state of politics in America. Pastel had very little to say, but seemed to be taking mental notes regarding what she was hearing, especially from Simone.

Over an after-dinner brandy, Simone declared that she hadn't spent such an enjoyable evening in many years. Sara seconded her comment, acknowledging that she had much to think about. Brendan joked that Sara and Simone might wind up as characters in his new novel. The three older adults then turned to Pastel, expecting her to remark on the evening.

"I know you're waiting for me to say something," she said, "but frankly I'm in a quandary. My two new friends represent two quite different role models. Simone has concentrated on her career and achieved considerable notoriety. Sara has focused on her family and been a wonderful wife, mother, and homemaker.

CHAPTER 13

FRIDAY, SEPTEMBER 23, 2022

Sara spent yet another restless night as the Argonaut sailed from Livorno to Marseille. This time night sweats weren't to blame. Sara couldn't stop thinking about the conversation at last evening's dinner, especially Brendan Greene's comment that some women resort to violence when they don't get what they desire while others simply decide to desire something different. Sara had never felt like reacting violently when she didn't become the artist she wanted to be, but that probably was because her dreams were not dashed all at once. They eroded slowly, sometimes imperceptibly, over time.

Perhaps if David one day had demanded that Sara abandon her plans to pursue art and focus on raising a family, she might have gotten her back up and reacted differently. But he never said a word about her aspirations. Instead, like a melting glacier, Sara's dreams of becoming an artist slowly slipped away, one interruption at a time. Throughout the process she continued to cling to her dreams until one day she didn't.

Before saying goodnight to Pastel after yesterday's stimulating dinner, Sara made plans for the two of them to travel together to Avignon once their ship reached port. Pastel's injured leg had improved, and she expressed an interest in seeing the walled city. Simone also was invited, but declined.

Despite waking up tired, Sara was excited about her upcoming excursion. She and David had enjoyed their two days in Avignon. With hot weather again forecast, she chose to wear shorts and a Hawaiian-style top that Randy sent her from Honolulu. She still couldn't believe he was meeting her in Barcelona tomorrow.

At breakfast, Sara ran into Pastel. They ate together and discussed their upcoming trip. Since her young friend had never visited Avignon before, Sara thought a visit to the papal palace was a must along with lunch in the old quarter. If time permitted, she recommended a tasting of the local Chateauneuf-du-Pape wine.

The conversation shifted to last night's dinner at La Boheme. "Did I embarrass you," Pastel asked, "when I mentioned that you and Simone are role models for me?"

"You certainly caught me by surprise, but I wasn't embarrassed. I must admit, however, that it can be disconcerting to hear someone acknowledge that I gave up my dream of becoming an artist in order to care for my family."

"I'm so sorry, Sara. I could tell my comment bothered you. I had no right to make it."

"Well, at least I was in the running for a role model with Simone. She's quite a force of nature. It would have been wonderful to meet her when she was younger and in good health."

"Did you ever have a role model when you were younger?" Pastel asked as she finished her omelet.

"In fact, I did. I wanted to be like Georgia O'Keefe."

"A rebel?"

"Definitely, but also more than that. Her life had no limits. She never allowed others to define her."

Sara could tell her comments struck a chord with Pastel, but breakfast wasn't the time or place for a serious discussion. The women agreed to meet in the departure lounge in half an hour.

"Be sure to bring sunscreen and a hat," Sara called out as they parted. Then she muttered under her breath, "Will I never give up mothering people?"

Sara considered checking on Simone, but didn't want to risk waking her. She'd stop by her room after the excursion. In the departure lounge, Sara asked the concierge about transportation to

Avignon. He advised her to take the high-speed TGV train, which covered the fifty-two miles in a mere thirty-three minutes, assuming, of course, French railroad workers didn't decide to call a spur-of-the-moment strike. Twenty-seven trains ran daily between Marseille and Avignon.

Pastel showed up a few minutes later wearing a youthful blue and yellow sundress, athletic shoes, and a New York Yankees baseball cap. The pair disembarked and caught a taxi to the railroad station. They arrived in Avignon soon thereafter. Sara regretted choosing the TGV because the beautiful countryside flew by so rapidly that she couldn't appreciate the farms, fields, and vineyards made famous by Impressionist painters. If time permitted, she planned to return to the ship by private car or bus.

A brief ride took Sara and Pastel from the TGV station to the center of Avignon. The women walked to the papal palace where they found a guide who conducted tours in English. Sara decided Pastel could have done just as good a job of guiding them, since she had gotten on-line after dinner and learned all about Pope Clement the Fifth's decision to relocate the papacy from Rome to Avignon. Sara forgot that Clement was French. According to Pastel, he felt safer in France than in Rome because warring factions in the fourteenth century made the Italian peninsula extremely dangerous.

Pastel reminded Sara of David because he always gathered background information before visiting new places. She recalled how he enjoyed answering tour guides' questions before anyone else in their group. Even more to his liking was actually correcting tour guides when he believed they got their facts wrong. This penchant for correction also managed to invade the Castle home. Sara, Randy, and Marie usually did not appreciate David's insistence on factual accuracy.

Once inside the papal palace, Sara remembered how few pieces of art were on display. Without paintings, tapestries, and statues, the place seemed uninviting and sterile. The presence of art made such a difference. When Sara shared this opinion with the tour guide, he pointed out that many of the objects that once adorned the palace either had been destroyed during the French Revolution or moved to the Petit Palais Museum nearby. Sara apologized to Pastel for not planning to visit the museum first before touring the papal palace.

Once the tour ended, Pastel desired to visit the famous St. Benezet Bridge, only a portion of which still stood above the Rhone River. The view of Avignon from the bridge was impressive, and Pastel took several photos with her cell phone and sent them to her father.

By the time the two women returned to the center of the old quarter, both were sweating and in need of shade and something cool to drink. An uncrowded café with patio tables under umbrellas was found. Sara asked Pastel to order something cool to drink while she went to the restroom.

When she returned, two wine spritzers sat on the table. Pastel commented that Sara seemed amused. Her visit to the restroom, she explained, brought back memories of a very playful moment during her honeymoon. Pastel insisted that Sara share the story.

"If you must know," Sara said with a laugh, "blame it on youthful lust and Avignon's romantic ambience. David couldn't keep his hands off me when we had lunch at a café very similar to this one. He kept touching me under the table, which got me aroused. After our second glass of wine, I finally told David to meet me in the restroom in three minutes. Despite the cramped surroundings, we had no trouble making love. I get excited now just remembering it. Imagine the surprised reaction we got from an elderly lady when she watched the two of us walk out of the restroom together."

"I thought that sort of thing just happened in x-rated movies," Pastel coyly commented.

"Well, we both enjoyed it. Unfortunately, the longer couples are together, the rarer such spontaneous moments of passion become. Enjoy them while you can."

Pastel seemed uncomfortable talking any further about sex. She suggested placing their orders for lunch. When the waiter showed up, both women requested salad nicoise. While they waited to be served, Sara told Pastel about Randy's surprise phone call and invitation to lunch in Barcelona. When Sara asked Pastel if she would like to join them, she readily accepted.

Having heard a voice she recognized, Sara suddenly turned around. At an adjacent café, she spotted Trevor Collins. A young woman appeared to be harassing him about something in French. The way the woman was dressed, Sara guessed she might be a prostitute.

Rising quickly from her chair, Sara walked over to where Trevor was seated, yelled at the woman in English, and motioned for her to go. She then took a seat beside Trevor, pretending to be his wife. A waiter appeared and apologized for the woman's rudeness. Once she was out of sight, Sara suggested Trevor join her and Pastel. Trevor paid his bill and left.

"I owe you one," he said gratefully. "She wouldn't leave me alone. I don't speak French very well, but I assumed she was offering herself to me."

"A good-looking man sitting by himself is a ready target for prostitutes," Sara pointed out. "I was surprised how bold she was."

"So, you think I'm good-looking," Trevor replied with a wink.

Sara blushed and introduced Pastel.

Trevor asked if they had visited the papal palace earlier. They nodded. He told them about spending the morning tasting vintage Chateauneuf-de-Pape at a well-known winery across the Rhone. "The best time to taste great wine is in the morning," he asserted. "Our taste buds are more receptive then."

Sara noted that she and Pastel planned to visit a winery before leaving Avignon, and Trevor asked if he could tag along, just in case more prostitutes accosted him. Both women laughed and responded that having a companion who knew about wine would be delightful.

The salads arrived, and Trevor ordered a glass of viognier. While the women ate, Trevor disclosed that his cabin attendant told him that several passengers on the Argonaut had to be quarantined because they tested positive for COVID.

"Can you imagine coming all this way only to be confined to your room? That could be grounds for mutiny," Sara declared.

"I know I'm not ready to resume wearing a mask all the time," Pastel added.

"My cabin attendant wasn't supposed to tell me about the COVID cases, but he knew I'm a diabetic. He recommended that I wear a mask when I'm on the ship."

While Sara and Pastel grazed on their salads, Trevor offered a mini-lecture on the history of Avignon's old quarter. The papal palace, he observed, had once been the most heavily fortified residence in Europe. Streets in Avignon often were named for the enterprises located on them. Examples included Hosiery Street, Street of the Golden Scissors, and Street of the Animal Furriers.

When lunch was finished, Trevor excused himself to visit the restroom. Pastel took the opportunity to ask Sara if she'd like to join Trevor in the restroom.

"I knew I shouldn't have shared that story," Sara replied.

Pastel laughed out loud. "Seriously, if you'd like some time alone with Trevor…"

Sara cut her off. "Just so you know, I'm not on this trip to find a replacement for David," she responded sharply, "nor do I think Trevor is looking to replace his wife." Sara immediately regretted snapping at Pastel.

When Trevor returned, Sara asked him to suggest a winery to visit. "We could cross the Rhone, as I did earlier, and visit a vineyard with a winery, but that might take more time than we can afford. I know a lovely tasting room several blocks from here where we can sample good wines from a variety of wineries."

"That sounds perfect," Sara replied. "Is it located on the Street of Winos?"

As the trio ambled to the tasting room, Trevor explained the make-up of a Rhone blend. The three main Rhone reds were syrah, grenache, and mourvedre. Wines from the northern Rhone were driven by syrah, while their southern cousins relied more on grenache. Sara observed that David preferred Bordeaux reds and loved sharing new discoveries with his friends.

The tasting room was dimly lit and resembled a cave. Racks of wine bottles lined the walls. A bar roughly ten feet long occupied the rear of the room, while a scattering of small tables with chairs filled the front. Behind the bar stood a short, balding man wearing a mask and an apron and drying wine glasses.

Trevor offered a "bon jour," which the man repeated three times in response. Trevor then spoke to him in French, which clearly pleased the man and impressed Sara. From what she could gather, Trevor requested several Rhone blends. The man, who introduced himself as Pierre, began selecting bottles and placing them along the bar.

Trevor studied each bottle as he explained to Sara and Pastel that he was comparing regions, vintages, and alcohol content. From the eight bottles presented by Pierre, Trevor chose four to be opened.

"Your husband, Madame, knows his wine," Pierre told Sara.

Sara smiled and replied, "Since you are French, Monsieur, you must know that men prefer to drink wine with their mistresses."

Pierre winked at Sara and said, "A thousand pardons, Madame. I assumed your young companion was your daughter."

At this point a middle-aged couple walked into the tasting room. Pierre moved the four bottles to one of the tables, then returned with three glasses and a dump bucket. Trevor asked for three additional glasses so they could do side-by-side tastings. He instructed his companions to notice the color and aroma of the wine before swirling and sipping.

An hour later, all four of the wines had been tasted and compared. Sara preferred the two southern Rhone blends, commenting that the cherry flavor of the grenache appealed to her. Trevor favored the two northern Rhone blends because of the savory quality of the syrah. Pastel expressed no preference, but looked as if she could fall asleep at any moment. Trevor requested bottled water so she could hydrate.

The middle-aged couple at the bar departed, and Pierre came over to inquire about the wines. When he noticed Pastel's groggy condition, he pivoted and went into a room behind the bar. A few minutes later he returned with a plate of cheese and baguette slices.

"You must eat a little," he instructed Pastel. Then he addressed Sara and Trevor. "Wine drinkers and wine are very similar. Each experiences infancy, youth, and finally maturity. This young woman is still in her infancy as a wine drinker."

Pastel looked up at Pierre. "Right now, I feel like I've reached the final stage – death."

After a while, the food and water took effect, and Pastel revived. Trevor asked her what she did back in the United States. She spoke about assisting her father with his manuscripts, then noted her desire also to be a writer.

"I, too, have thought about writing now that I'm retired. I don't know what the attraction is. Maybe we just want to leave part of ourselves behind. My great idea was to write a book about the similarities between designing a building and designing a life."

"Have you ever done it?" Pastel asked.

"Not yet, but there's always the possibility that I'll buckle down one day and write it."

Sara nodded in agreement. "It's all about discipline, isn't it? That's what I've lacked, the discipline to get back to painting."

Pierre had been following the conversation and quipped, "This is why we have wine. Discipline is never enough. We must also be creative. Creativity and wine go together like Bardot and bikinis."

"I don't feel very creative at the moment," Pastel chimed in, "and I've had plenty of wine."

Sara checked the time and suggested that they settle the bill and catch a taxi back to the ship.

"Can I join you?" Trevor said. "I'll be glad to cover the cost."

"How about we share the cost?"

When Pierre returned with the bill for the wine, he announced that a wine shipment was waiting in Marseille to be picked up. "I'd be glad to have your company for the trip. It's a slow day here, so I can close the shop. I know where the cruise ships dock. It's not a very long trip."

Pierre locked up the tasting room, and the quartet walked a block to the small lot where his commercial minivan was parked. During the drive to Marseille, Pierre spoke of his dream to one day own a vineyard. Then he added, "But before one can grow grapes, he must raise a family to help with planting, pruning, and harvesting. My Sylvia, bless her heart, cannot bear children, so I must sell the wine from other people's vineyards."

"Just be thankful your Sylvia can bear you," Trevor responded.

Sara found his comment puzzling. She wondered if it reflected Trevor's relationship with his deceased wife. There was something about the man that intrigued Sara, but she had trouble identifying it. She normally found men transparent, easy to figure out. Most desired the same things in life: opportunities to achieve, recognition for their achievements, undemanding companionship, and regular sex. Whatever Trevor's desires were, she had yet to discover them.

When the group reached the dock area in Marseille, Sara thanked Pierre, gave him a hug, and offered him money. He kissed her lightly on each cheek and refused to accept the money, insisting that the company was more than sufficient payment. Trevor helped Pastel, who had slept for most of the trip, maneuver unsteadily out of the mini-van, and the trio went through the passport check point. After climbing the gangplank, Pastel announced that she intended to take a nap. Trevor invited Sara to dine with him later in the evening.

"I would enjoy having dinner with you as long as Simone is all right. I promised to check on her when I returned from Avignon. If you don't hear from me, I'll meet you at the Pathfinder Dining Room. Shall we say seven o'clock?"

"Perfect. I'll reserve a table. Will two do?"

"A table for two will be fine."

When Simone opened the door, Sara immediately knew her friend was having a bad day. Her voice and posture conveyed the pain she was suffering. Short breaths punctuated her halting speech. Unable to eat anything since the previous evening, Simone admitted feeling weak and a little dizzy.

"We need to see the ship's physician," Sara declared.

Simone shook her head and retreated to the sofa. "I can't risk being transferred off the ship and into a hospital. I must get to Lisbon, Sara."

"What's so important about Lisbon? I realize you spent time there with Amadou, but isn't your health more important at the moment?" Sara suspected Simone was keeping something from her.

Simone complained of being very thirsty, so Sara poured her a glass of water from the bottle provided by the cabin attendant. After taking several sips, Simone set down her glass and pressed the palms of her hands against her eyes and forehead. "Most of my life has been spent working with words, but I can't find the words to describe the pain I'm feeling now."

Sara sat beside Simone and put an arm around her. She acknowledged having taken pain medication just before Sara arrived. "It takes twenty minutes to kick in," Simone said as she rested her head on Sara's shoulder.

Sara picked up the room phone. "I'm going to order room service for you. Pain or no pain, you must eat something. I can tell you're very weak. You can't fight cancer on an empty stomach."

When she reached the cabin attendant, Sara asked what was available for in-room dining. She eventually chose turkey and mashed potatoes. "Think of it as an early Thanksgiving dinner," Sara joked.

While they waited for room service to arrive, Sara told Simone about what she and Pastel did in Avignon and how they ran into Trevor. Learning that his cabin attendant disclosed there were some COVID cases on board, Simone became alarmed.

"Sara, I've got to get off this ship. I can't risk catching COVID and having to quarantine. You know I'm especially susceptible, given my condition." Once again, Simone stressed the necessity of reaching Lisbon.

"I don't want to risk having to quarantine either," Sara agreed. "You're safe as long as you get room service and avoid the crowded dining areas."

"You can't know that, Sara. I could catch COVID from my cabin attendant or from you, for that matter. My only hope is to get off this ship."

"I can't do anything tomorrow. Pastel and I are meeting my son, Randy, for lunch in Barcelona. Let me think about what we can do if we leave the ship. Day after tomorrow we stop in Almeria, Spain. Promise me you won't do anything rash, and I'll promise to come up with a plan."

Simone swore she would wait until Sara had a chance to think about options. Sara remained with Simone until dinner arrived and then went to her own room. The first thing Sara did was get on-line and look up information on pancreatic cancer and its treatment. Then she showered, changed into a short-sleeved dress and pumps, and went to meet Trevor. Sara reflected on how long it used to take her to get ready to go out with David and how much she had shortened her prep time.

Before checking on Simone, Sara had anticipated steering dinner conversation toward Trevor's plans for the future. Now, however, she was too preoccupied with Simone's pain and her obsession with reaching Lisbon. Trevor sensed Sara's thoughts were elsewhere and asked if she wished to share them. How novel, she noted to herself, for a man to be so intuitive.

After listening to Sara relate her visit with Simone, Trevor got his cell phone and started searching for something. He asked her to order drinks for them. A few minutes later he reported that Lisbon was less than a nine-hour drive from Almeria. The route ran past Granada, Seville, and Albufeira.

"So, I could drive Simone to Lisbon if we disembarked at Almeria," Sara announced.

"Just call ahead and reserve a rental car that can be dropped off in Lisbon. Would you like for me to go with you? I could help with the driving."

"You are such a gentleman, Trevor. That's a lovely offer, but I'm going to ask Pastel to join us. We'll need the back seat for Simone, in case she needs to lie down."

"I understand. Here's a way I can help, however. The three of you can't possibly fit all your luggage from the ship in one car. Each of you could pack an overnight bag for the trip. The rest of your luggage can be left with me, and I'll make sure it gets unloaded in Lisbon."

For the remainder of dinner Sara couldn't stop thanking Trevor for his suggestions and generosity. When he escorted her back to her room, she gave him a hug. She really felt like adding a kiss, but could not quite bring herself to do so.

Entering her room, Sara greeted David's framed photograph and related how she had re-visited the papal palace in Avignon and remembered their romantic restroom rendezvous. She undressed and went to bed, but that night her dreams were not of David.

CHAPTER 14

SATURDAY, SEPTEMBER 24, 2022

Sara's brain was like an overstuffed in-basket when she awakened on Saturday. Much of the night had been spent sifting through a variety of impending matters. She hadn't seen her son since before the Pandemic. Did he have important news to share? What would she tell him about? Then there was the plan she and Trevor concocted to drive Simone to Lisbon and avoid the possibility of contracting COVID on the Argonaut. Both Simone and Pastel needed to be notified. Time would be required to prepare an overnight bag and pack up the rest of their luggage for Trevor to handle. Finally, there was Trevor. He certainly didn't represent a serious relationship in her mind, but the potential might be there. Was it too soon to consider such things?

Once she was fully awake and dressed, Sara called Simone. When she shared the plans for a Portuguese pilgrimage, Simone's voice rose an octave or two. "Praise be to God," she called out. Sara pictured Simone's Aunt Pearl delivering the same words in church on Sundays. Before ending the call, Sara suggested that they have dinner tonight with Pastel and Trevor in order to go over final details.

The next phone call was to Pastel, first to arrange a meeting for their trip into Barcelona to meet Randy and second to fill her in on the plan to take Simone to Lisbon. When she heard about the latter, Pastel immediately agreed to go. She had recently learned of additional COVID cases on board the Argonaut from her father. Hearing this, Sara reconsidered her dinner plans and suggested it might be safer for the four of them to order room service. They could gather in her room, since it was larger than Simone's or Pastel's.

"What about Trevor's room," Pastel said with a giggle.

"I wouldn't know, you nosey wench," Sara responded.

Sara called Simone again to fill her in on the change of plans and then got in touch with Trevor to let him know. When he didn't answer, she left a voicemail message. Despite realizing it was none of her business, Sara couldn't help wondering where Trevor might be at that hour of the morning.

Heather McKay, the ship's activity director, announced over the intercom that the ship would be docking in Barcelona within the hour. She recommended wearing summer attire because the temperature was expected to be in the eighties. Sara changed her mind about wearing nice jeans and a light blouse in favor of a sundress and sandals.

After grabbing a latte and cinnamon bun, Sara visited the concierge to get directions to Els Quatre Gats. When Pastel met her in the departure lounge, she suggested visiting La Sagrada Familia on their way to lunch. Sara admitted having the same idea. She told Pastel that she and David saw Gaudi's remarkable, but still unfinished, church on their honeymoon.

"I imagine there have been many changes to the church in three decades," Sara commented. "I'd love to see how close to completion it is."

"I've read that some people believe it will never be completed," Pastel replied.

"Did you know Trevor was an architect?" Sara asked. "I'll bet he plans on visiting La Sagrada Familia while the ship is in Barcelona."

Pastel flashed a smile, but did not reply.

Given the large number of passengers leaving the ship to sight-see in Barcelona, it took a while for Sara and Pastel to find a taxi into the city. They were careful to keep their masks on until the crowd dispersed. After finally catching a ride, Sara shared what she had found out about pancreatic cancer as the driver threaded her way through the busy streets.

"Simone had me believing that little could be done about her condition, but the more I read, the more I came to realize that she might have treatment options that could extend her life. I have a feeling she'd qualify for surgery to remove the cancer if she just gained some weight. Even if the cancer has advanced too far to be removed, palliative surgery can relieve some of her intense pain. The surgery involves unblocking the bile ducts that tend to become clogged."

"So, you think there's a chance Simone could get better?"

"I'm certainly not an expert, but it sounds like there's a possibility she could live longer with less pain. The problem, as I see it, is that Simone has made up her mind she's going to die sooner rather than later."

"Why do you think that?"

"Because she doesn't seem to have any compelling reason to go on living."

"Then we need to give her one," Pastel insisted.

Just as Pastel declared her desire to help Simone, the majestic spires of La Sagrada Familia came into view. Sara asked the driver to let them out across the street from the church. As Sara was paying the driver, she warned that it was impossible to see the entire church in one day. She added her hope that their friend would get better. Sara hadn't realized the driver spoke enough English to follow the conversation.

"When David and I visited, he could not believe that one man had the imagination to design such a structure. After seeing the church and then strolling through Park Guell, David was overwhelmed by Gaudi's genius. I recall telling him that artists think differently from other people. They see things as they can be, not just as they are."

Pastel frowned. "My mother, as you know, is an artist, but I'm not so sure she can see things as they can be. She certainly didn't exhibit her artistic imagination when it came to her marriage or my upbringing."

Pastel's comment caused Sara to wonder what kind of parent she would have been if she pursued her art career after marrying David. The two women started to walk around the perimeter of La Sagrada Familia. Suddenly Sara called out, "I told you so."

Pastel looked baffled.

"Over there, near the line at the entrance." Sara pointed in that direction.

Pastel turned, spotted Trevor, and waved. He smiled and returned her wave. Even though it meant losing his place in line, Trevor came over to greet the pair.

"Sara bet we'd probably run into you here," Pastel announced.

"I didn't realize I was that predictable."

"You are an architect, after all," Sara asserted. "I can't imagine you'd miss this masterpiece."

"Just to be accurate, I'm a retired architect. Perhaps if I'd been blessed with Gaudi's gifts, I'd still be practicing."

"You've certainly set a high bar for yourself," Sara replied. "What can you tell us about La Sagrada Familia?"

The three began to stroll around the outside of the church as Trevor pointed to key features of Gaudi's design. Each spire, he noted, was dedicated to a different religious figure from the New Testament. The overall architectural style combined Gothic and Art Nouveau elements. The structure located at the southern corner of the church used to be at the eastern corner. Gaudi originally intended the building to house a school for the children of construction workers involved in erecting the edifice.

Eventually the three arrived back at the entrance, where the line of people waiting to get in still extended a full city block or more. Sara apologized for needing to leave, explaining that she and Pastel had a luncheon date with her son.

"I almost forgot," she exclaimed. "Did you get my phone message about meeting for dinner this evening?"

"I was at the fitness center when you called. Yes, I'd love to meet and discuss your escape plan. I agree that it's better to meet in your room than risk catching COVID in a dining area. While I'm in town I'll pick up a nice Priorat for dinner.

"What a splendid idea. Don't forget to order room service and have it delivered to my room. Why don't we get together at seven o'clock."

Trevor walked over to the street and hailed a taxi for Sara and Pastel. The driver spoke no English, but recognized El Quatre Gats. The women waved goodbye to Trevor as Pastel commented, "What a gentleman he is. And so knowledgeable about Gaudi and his church. I wish he were younger or I was older."

Sara almost responded that she was the perfect age for Trevor, but decided that might be misinterpreted.

"Did you eat at the Four Cats on your honeymoon?" Pastel asked.

"We did. I had insisted we go, despite David's reluctance to be surrounded by artsy types, as he called people like me. The cafe had been a watering hole for writers and artists during Catalonia's modernist period. I still can recall sitting at a corner table drinking espresso and envisioning what the atmosphere must have been like at the end of the nineteenth century. Though I wasn't a smoker, I even asked David for a cigarette so I could feel more a part of the café crowd."

"Do you think David enjoyed the experience?"

"You know, Pastel, it probably sounds silly, but I could never be quite certain whether David appreciated doing things that I wanted to do or simply tolerated my interests out of affection for me. I had hoped we would discuss serious, worldly issues as we dined, but all David wanted to do was plan the next day's activities."

The taxi driver pulled up at a corner in the old quarter and gestured down the street. Traffic had snarled, and apparently, he could not or would not try to get closer to El Quatre Gats. Pastel figured out what they owed and paid the driver. The women walked a block to the cafe.

Upon entering the establishment, Sara's eyes suddenly lit up. "Randy," she called out. A tall, fair-haired man in an airline pilot's uniform rose from a corner table to greet her.

"I can't believe you're really here and sitting in the exact spot where your father and I sat on our honeymoon." Sara gave Randy a hug.

"It's been far too long, Mom. I'm so thankful COVID restrictions are starting to ease some." Randy noticed Pastel approaching and said, "And who have we here?"

"Allow me to introduce Pastel Greene," Sara replied with a warm smile.

"Anticipating Randy's predictable response, Pastel spoke first. "I know. My mother is an artist. I could have shortened my name to Paste, but that didn't sound very good either."

Randy laughed and pulled up a chair for Pastel. The threesome chatted as they waited for a server. Sara asked about Randy's flight and when he had to return to the U.S. Pastel wondered if Randy had dealt with more unruly passengers since the Pandemic began. Randy inquired about what Pastel did back home and how she was liking the cruise.

The server, a middle-aged man who bore a striking resemblance to Ernest Hemingway, eventually arrived and asked for drink orders. Pastel and Sara opted for Cava while Randy ordered a double espresso. An alcoholic beverage, he feared, would put him to sleep.

By the time drinks arrived, the conversation had shifted to more personal topics. Randy wanted to know how Sara felt about Marie, Marcus, and Parker moving to Charlotte and whether she planned to sell her own house and find something smaller.

"Honestly, Randy, I haven't had much time to think about it. I only learned about the move just before going on the cruise. Since your father died, I haven't been motivated to do any serious planning. Going on the cruise was the biggest decision I've made in a very long time."

"That reminds me," Randy interjected, "how come you didn't book a return ticket? I checked your flight arrangements because I wanted to treat you to a first-class seat on your trip home."

"What a sweet gesture, Randy. I appreciate your thoughtfulness. Frankly, when I purchased my ticket, I couldn't think of a good reason to return immediately after the cruise ended. So, for once in my life, Miss Practical chose to do something uncharacteristic."

"That's very interesting," Pastel chimed in. "Simone told me she didn't book a return ticket either. Maybe the two of you can explore Portugal for a while. You could even sign up for art lessons. I'm sure Lisbon has a place to study art."

"I remember how you used to talk about your love of art," Randy added. "I know you majored in fine arts in college. Marie and I were amazed at the sketches of us that you used to draw. What happened?"

"The short answer is life happened." Sara avoided looking at Randy. "I fell in love with David."

"You're still youngish, Mom. Look at Grandma Moses. It's not too late to pursue your dreams."

"Perhaps I could, but I recall when your father decided to take up golf because it was a way to meet potential donors. He arranged for lessons, joined a private club, and bought an expensive set of golf clubs. Your father, however, was a perfectionist. He never could shoot as well as he wanted to, and he blamed it on getting too late a start. I suspect I'd make a similar discovery if I began to paint again."

The server returned with drinks and asked for lunch orders. Randy selected the arros caldos, while Sara and Pastel agreed to split the paella.

Pastel, who hadn't said much, turned to Randy and asked, "How would you feel if your mother met a man she liked?"

Sara gave Pastel a hard stare that screamed, "What were you thinking?"

"Thank you for asking, Pastel. I'm sure Mom wouldn't have. My sister might have issues with Mom dating, but I think it would be great. There's no reason she shouldn't enjoy life to the fullest. I know she's earned it."

"What issues do you think Marie might have?" Sara inquired.

"You know as well as I do that Marie has trouble dealing with change. She worships predictability. If you were to meet a man you cared for, I'm not sure Marie could accept him."

"With her upcoming move to Charlotte, Marie will have plenty of changes to keep her busy," Sara responded.

Lunch concluded with lemon sorbet, crema catalana, and coffee. Sara and Pastel told Randy about Simone and their plan to leave the ship and drive her to Lisbon. Much to Pastel's surprise, Sara also mentioned Trevor. Randy asked for Pastel's cell phone number and promised to call if he had a layover in New York. Then he picked up the check and said it was time for him to get some rest before his return flight.

Sara hugged Randy. "I can't tell you how much it meant to see you again. I hope it won't be another two years before we see each other."

"Thanksgiving is coming up. If you're not still hanging out in Lisbon, maybe I can get down to Charlottesville. I'll check my flight schedule and let you know."

"That would be a truly worthy reason to give thanks. Perhaps I can convince Pastel to join us."

Not much was said during the taxi ride back to the port. Once the driver was paid and departed, however, Pastel grabbed Sara's arm before she entered the re-boarding checkpoint. "Can I ask you a personal question?"

"Of course. It's about Randy, isn't it?"

Pastel blushed, but shook her head.

"Well, just for the record, I think he really likes you."

"I know we only just met, but I really like him as well. Here's my question. What's the real reason you didn't pursue your dream of becoming an artist? You told Randy it was because you fell in love with David, but my intuition says there's more to it than that."

Sara looked at Pastel, then looked away. "I'd say your intuition is pretty good." She guided Pastel from the line of re-boarding passengers and over to an unoccupied bench.

"What I'm going to tell you must never be shared with Randy or with Marie, if you ever meet her. Agreed?"

"Agreed."

"When I met David in my fourth year at the University of Virginia, he was in graduate school. We liked each other and went out on several dates, but I also was dating someone else. I'm embarrassed to say that I got pregnant, but I wasn't sure who the father was."

Pastel's eyes grew big. "Did you consider terminating the pregnancy?"

"I did not. You see, I cared for both David and Michael. Sara the Practical decided that Michael, who was still an undergraduate, was in no position to become a father, even if the baby turned out to be his. David, on the other hand, impressed me as being very responsible and ambitious. I knew he'd make a good father."

"So, what did you do?"

"I told David the truth, that I was pregnant, but unsure who the father was. He took it amazingly well, all things considered. To my surprise, he believed the two of us would make great parents and suggested that we get married as soon as possible. After such a noble gesture, I knew that I could learn to love David. I also understood that his career would have to come first. He deserved that concession given how unselfish he had been. I still feel it was the right thing to do."

"This sounds like the prelude to a really amazing novel," Pastel confided as she wiped away a few tears. "Did you ever determine the actual father?"

"We agreed it was not something we needed to know. A small wedding was held a month before the baby was due. My family was aware of our situation, but they weren't bothered or upset about it. Both felt I was fortunate to marry such a wonderful man. The sad part of the story is that the baby was stillborn. Years later when Randy and Marie arrived, my parents and David's parents agreed that there was no reason to share the story with them. Neither one knows how David and I really wound up together."

As the two women stood up to re-board the Argonaut, Pastel grabbed Sara's arm. "Were you serious about inviting me for Thanksgiving in Charlottesville?"

"Absolutely serious. Who knows where such an invitation might lead?" Sara winked.

After re-boarding the Argonaut, the two women headed to their rooms to pack overnight bags for the upcoming drive from Almeria to Lisbon. Pastel volunteered to check on Simone and remind her of the dinner meeting in Sara's room at seven. Once again, Pastel stopped Sara with a query.

"After David's tragic accident, did you ever attempt to reconnect with the person you were before the two of you married?"

"That's an odd question. Why do you ask?"

"I read somewhere about a study that followed a large number of individuals from the time they were in college until they were in their seventies. The researchers discovered that most of the subjects in their teenage years possessed an important dream for the future. Practically all of them admitted setting aside their dream as they confronted the predictable challenges of adulthood, like finding a job, getting married, starting a family, addressing health issues, and so on."

"Was that their major finding? I could have told them that and saved them the trouble."

"Let me finish. In their later years, some of the participants reported feeling fulfilled and upbeat about their lives. Others, however, looked back on their lives with regret and sadness. You want to know what distinguishes the two groups?"

"Of course I do. Please enlighten me."

"The group that regarded their lives more positively found ways to reconnect in later life with their youthful dreams. The others were unable or unwilling to resurrect and pursue those dreams."

"I'll bet the first group were men," Sara commented.

"You're correct," Pastel answered, "but so were the second group. No women were in the study."

"Too much food for thought," Sara laughed. "I'm going on a diet."

Later that evening the "escape" planners met in Sara's room. Simone appeared to be more upbeat than the day before. Trevor opened one of the Priorats that he bought in Barcelona. Servers soon arrived with meals the diners had ordered from room service. The room filled with the smells of garlic, spices, and fresh bread.

Pastel encouraged Simone to finish all of her lobster ravioli so she'd have enough energy for tomorrow's drive.

Sara reported that the concierge helped her locate an SUV rental in Almeria. The Argonaut was expected to dock around eight the next morning, and the travelers agreed to be ready to leave the ship by nine. Trevor requested that any luggage remaining on the ship should be dropped off at his room by seven thirty in the morning. He promised to have all the suitcases transferred to the Lisbon ship terminal, where they could be picked up on Tuesday.

"Does anyone have a problem stopping in Granada to see the Alhambra?" Sara asked. "I have wonderful honeymoon memories of my visit with David."

"Count me in," Pastel enthusiastically responded.

"The Alhambra is breathtaking," Simone added. "Amadou took me there. As long as we get to Lisbon by Tuesday, I'm fine with stops along the way."

"Can you tell us what awaits you in Lisbon," Pastel asked. "I, for one, am dying to know."

"All in due time, my inquisitive young friend."

Sara went on to explain that stopping in Granada and possibly going on to Seville to spend the night would be a good way to break up the trip. The entire trip from Almeria to Lisbon, she added, would take around eight to ten hours, depending on traffic. Barring any unexpected delays, they should reach Lisbon by Monday afternoon.

Explaining that she still had some packing to do, Simone excused herself. After a second glass of wine, Pastel also departed to check on her father and let him know about her plan to travel by land to Lisbon.

Alone now with Trevor, Sara thought about the study Pastel mentioned about men and their youthful dreams. She summarized the study, then asked Trevor what he had dreamed of becoming when he was a teenager.

"I was serious when I told you in Taormina that I wanted to be a professional golfer. My father introduced me to the game, and I loved it. I played in high school and got a scholarship to play in college."

"So, what happened?"

"In my sophomore year I was playing in a tournament in Louisiana. I had a low score going to the fifteenth hole on the last day of competition. My drive landed several feet from a tree. I had enough room to swing for the green, so I selected my five iron and swung. My club came into contact with a root just below where the ball sat. I tore the tendons in my wrist and lower right arm. That was it for my golf career."

"That's awful, Trevor. I'm so sorry."

"Dad owned an architectural firm and suggested I transfer to the architecture school. I can't complain. Designing places for people to live and work and have fun has been reasonably satisfying. Like anything else, of course, it also involved frustrations and disappointments."

"Still, architecture was not your dream career."

"No, it was not what I dreamed of doing."

"Could it be that dreams are overrated?"

"Could it be that you'd like to believe that dreams are overrated?"

Sara smiled. "You're very intuitive, my friend."

"Well, it's getting late, and you've got a trip tomorrow. I'd better let you get some sleep."

Sara didn't want the evening to end, especially on a sad note. If she were entirely truthful, she wouldn't have minded for Trevor to stay the night. No one would know. He could return to his room early in the morning to receive Simone and Pastel's luggage.

Once again, however, the inner voice of Sara the Practical spoke up. Trevor probably is still hurting from his wife's untimely death. Does an individual ever fully recover from such a horrible tragedy? Am I not still mourning the loss of David?

Sara thanked Trevor for the wine, wheeled out the suitcase she wished to leave with him, and kissed him lightly on the cheek. Sleep would offer ample opportunity to reflect on might-have-beens.

CHAPTER 15

SUNDAY, SEPTEMBER 25, 2022

Instead of dreaming about might-have-beens, Sara spent a generous portion of the night worrying that her off-hand remark about seeing the Alhambra on her honeymoon with David had sent an unintended message to Trevor. She hoped her kiss had sent a different signal.

A second source of nocturnal uneasiness involved Simone. Was she really too frail to tour the Alhambra? The temperature clearly was too hot for her to wait in the rental vehicle. Then there was the mystery surrounding Simone's need to reach Lisbon. It nagged Sara like a poison ivy itch. Since Pastel revealed that Simone had not purchased a return plane ticket, what exactly did she plan to do in Lisbon?

Arising unrested was becoming routine. Sara got up at six thirty, showered and dressed, then asked her room attendant to bring coffee and a bagel with cream cheese. While she waited, Sara called Trevor and asked him to notify the registration desk, once the trio left the ship, of their decision to drive to Lisbon. Any outstanding bills could be charged to the credit card each woman registered with the bursar when they boarded.

Before hanging up, Sara asked Trevor if he was heading back to the United States immediately after the Argonaut reached Lisbon. He admitted having planned to catch a flight on Tuesday when the ship docked, but then acknowledged having second thoughts about returning so quickly. Sara sensed he was waiting for her to suggest that they spend a few days seeing what Lisbon had to offer, but she hesitated because of uncertainty over Simone's plans. Pastel, she assumed, would assist her father on his trip home.

Once the Argonaut docked in Almeria, the three women donned their masks and prepared to disembark. Sara and Simone carried medium-sized gym bags, while Pastel shouldered a backpack. Sara cautioned her friends not to bring any large liquid containers which could arouse suspicions when they reached the customs desk.

The car rental agency recommended by the concierge was located within walking distance of the port. Sara insisted on carrying Simone's bag once they cleared customs. Fortunately, morning fog still settled on the port area, making the temperature tolerable for the travelers.

At the rental agency, Sara produced her reservation confirmation and reminded the clerk that the SUV would be dropped off in Lisbon. Hearing this, the clerk frowned and stepped away from the counter to speak to an associate. The two spoke in Spanish for several minutes. When the clerk returned to the counter, he informed Sara that the original rental fee was incorrect. The actual fee was double the original amount.

At this point Pastel stepped up to the counter and addressed the clerk in Spanish. He turned beet red and apologized to Sara in English. The original charge would be honored, he said. The paperwork was completed, and the women were escorted to their vehicle, a burgundy BMW SUV that looked like it just rolled off the assembly line. Once the clerk left, Sara asked Pastel what she said to him at the counter.

"I overheard the two of them discussing the rental fee. The other guy must have been the manager. He advised our guy to double the charge. I simply told him that we had proof of the original quoted fee and that it had to be honored or I would report him to the Spanish authorities and the U.S. consulate."

"Bravo, young lady," Simone exclaimed. "We are indebted to

you. It's a comfort to know we'll have your language proficiency on the trip to Lisbon."

"I can only help in Spain, since I don't speak Portuguese."

After depositing the luggage in the rear of the SUV, Sara helped Simone stretch out on the back seat. A pillow "borrowed" from the Argonaut was positioned behind Simone to make the ride more comfortable. Sara checked the map provided by the rental agency and announced that Granada was roughly a hundred and seventy kilometers from Almeria. She estimated they would arrive a little after noon.

While Sara focused on negotiating Almeria's streets, Pastel picked up her cell phone and began reading text messages. Simone softly hummed a tune that was unfamiliar to Sara. Eventually the highway was reached, and the SUV sailed along past vast stretches of greenhouses, orchards, grape vines, and solar panels.

After Pastel put away her cell phone, Sara asked if she received any interesting text messages. She didn't acknowledge wondering if Randy had tried to reach Pastel.

"Just the usual stuff," Pastel replied. "Nothing gossip-worthy. Simone, are you still awake?"

"I am awake. Also woke up."

"I've been meaning to ask if you would allow me to interview you about your life. You've told us about your youth, but not much about your academic career."

"And what is the purpose of your proposed interrogation?"

"I'd like to write an article or maybe even a book about your life; that is, if you'd grant me permission to do so."

"What a grand idea," Sara chimed in.

Simone consented to answer any questions she might have, so Pastel retrieved a notepad and pen from her backpack. Her first question concerned Simone's area of specialization. Sara listened with great interest as Simone explained that her early work focused on African-American writers and artists who spent time in France after the First World War. The fact that Simone's mother abandoned her for an uncertain life in Paris, Sara assumed, played a role in this choice.

Some of the individuals that Simone investigated had been prominent figures associated with the Harlem Renaissance. Jean Toomer, in particular, intrigued Simone because he did not always identify with being Black and his thinking evolved significantly over time. Unlike many of his peers, Toomer embraced a multi-racial identity, foreshadowing the advent of legal marriages between the races. Simone believed that one of her most influential works had examined the possibility that a multi-racial society might undermine the development of a distinctive African-American culture.

Simone was on a roll now. She told Pastel about her fascination with left-wing Black writers, including Claude McKay, who became enamored of Communism during the thirties. What had attracted these talented individuals to the so-called dictatorship of the proletariat while others, like Jean Toomer, became associated with the teachings of spiritualists? As she eavesdropped, Sara realized how little she knew about Black history.

At times Sara became so absorbed in what Simone was saying that she lost track of where she was going. The challenges of scholarly investigation seemed so different from those faced by artists. Sara intended to ask Simone to recommend one of her books to read.

When Sara reached the outskirts of Granada, Simone asked for a bathroom break and something to eat. Pastel spotted a hotel, and Sara pulled into the parking lot. Having exchanged dollars for euros the previous day, Simone gave her friends coins in case there was a fee for using the toilets. All agreed that a light snack rather than a full lunch would be sufficient.

Back in the SUV, Pastel directed Sara to the immense grounds of the Alhambra. Simone acknowledged that she wasn't up to a full tour of the hilltop fortress and palace. She instead planned on going to the smaller and more charming summer palace. Escaping the midday heat would be easier there. Besides, she added, her best Spanish memories with Amadou occurred in the gardens of the emir's summer retreat. Pastel agreed to accompany Simone in case she required assistance. Before the trio split up, Sara bought bottled water for everyone and asked the summer palace contingent to return to the parking lot by three o'clock.

It pleased Sara that Pastel volunteered to go with Simone. She welcomed the opportunity to stretch her legs and enjoy some time on her own. While waiting in line to purchase a ticket, she tried to envision her earlier visit with David. The first image that came to mind was David complaining after the tour about a painful blister on his foot.

Sara's favorite recollection of Granada, in fact, did not involve the Alhambra at all, but instead a magical flamenco performance in a gypsy cave across the valley from the palace. Sara had no trouble picturing that enchanting evening. The cave, no more than fifteen feet wide and a hundred feet long, was lined on each side with simple chairs. A lone dancer dressed in a flowing red and black dress that almost reached the ground appeared unannounced from the rear of the dimly lit cave. An elderly guitarist slowly walked behind her.

No one spoke as the dancer commenced to dip and whirl to the dramatic chords of the guitar. Frequently she tapped the heels of her shoes so hard that Sara could feel the reverberations in her own feet. Moving back and forth between the rows of chairs, she came within inches of touching her seated guests. Somehow, she never made contact. David called it an erotic tease. She was so close, yet so distant. Occasionally her dark eyes locked the gaze of a spellbound guest for a split second, just long enough for the person to understand that they were privileged to be in the dancer's company. All the while the guitarist expressed his encouragement with guttural grunts and plaintive moans.

At times both the dancer's arms were raised above her head as she clicked her castanets to the rhythm of the guitar. At other times her right hand held up the hem of her dress so guests could appreciate her vigorous footwork. Twice during the evening, the dancer was joined by a slender man dressed in black. Sara thought their carefully coordinated movements were the most romantic thing she'd ever seen. Their dances offered proof, in Sara's mind, that it was possible to have sex while fully clothed. The memory still aroused her all these years later.

By the time the flamenco performance ended, performers and guests were sweating. The performers departed, but guests remained seated as if in a trance, captives of the experience. Eventually Sara and David wandered out of the cave, hand-in-hand. Back in their hotel room, the newly-weds' love making was unusually passionate. The following morning, Sara joked with David that he must have been thinking of the flamenco dancer.

The ticket seller for tours of the Alhambra broke Sara's reverie when she asked how many tickets were needed. Sara purchased one and joined a small group with an English-speaking guide, but a little later she decided to wander off on her own. As impressive as the architecture and mosaics were, Sara struggled to focus because her imagination remained riveted to the flamenco performance.

After ambling aimlessly for an hour, Sara left the Alhambra. It was only two-thirty, so when she spotted a fortune teller's tent near the parking lot, Sara decided to have her fortune told. Wouldn't it be fitting, she thought, if the fortune teller lived in one of the gypsy caves across the valley?

The woman appeared to be in her late forties. Inside the tent, her olive skin glistened in the candlelight. Her dark eyes and black eye liner reminded Sara of the flamenco dancer. The fortune teller's long black hair was pulled back from her face by a scarf. A scar crossed her left cheek. When Sara asked if she spoke English, the woman snapped, "When I must."

"What do you charge to read a fortune?" Sara inquired.

"You are a well-to-do woman. It should not matter."

Sara was taken aback by the woman's bluntness. She started to leave, but curiosity overrode annoyance.

The small circular table separating the fortune teller from Sara contained no crystal ball, only a frayed green cloth with gold tassels. The woman instructed Sara to place both hands, palms up, on the cloth. Then she asked the reason for Sara's visit.

"To be honest, I'm not sure why I'm here," Sara admitted.

"You are waiting for others to arrive."

The fortune teller's comment startled Sara. The tent had not been up when she arrived with Simone and Pastel. Sara decided the comment was a lucky guess.

After studying Sara's palms for several moments, the fortune teller said, "You are here because of a man."

"Is that why I'm here?" Sara silently asked herself. "Probably another lucky guess. When a woman wants her fortune told, nine times out of ten it likely involves a man. But in my case, which man?"

Before Sara could say anything, the fortune teller declared, "There is a new man in your life." The woman never took her eyes off Sara, making her feel uneasy. Sara looked down at her ring finger and noticed her wedding ring wasn't there. Then she remembered having removed it before going swimming near Taormina. For some reason that presently eluded her, Sara neglected to put the ring back on.

"The fortune teller probably assumed I was single," Sara thought. "And she can see that I'm not young. Okay, so the odds are great I came here because of a man. What do I want her to tell me?"

Once again, the fortune teller anticipated Sara's thoughts. "I cannot tell if you are meant to be with this man, but I know that you are uncertain about the relationship. What I can tell you is this."

Sara leaned forward.

"There can be no peace where there is desire."

"That's it?" Sara asked.

The fortune teller said nothing more, but held out her open hand. Sara still didn't know what the woman charged, but she reached in her purse and got a ten euro note Simone had given her. When she placed it in the woman's hand, the fortune teller looked neither pleased nor offended. Sara stood up and left.

As she walked away, Sara considered the fortune teller's parting words and decided she probably told everyone the same thing.

When Simone and Pastel returned to the parking lot a half hour later, Sara was anxious to share her brief meeting with the fortune teller, but Simone spoke first. "Our young friend had a slight meltdown at the summer palace."

"It is terribly hot," Sara replied.

"It had nothing to do with the temperature," Pastel answered.

"I asked Simone about her visit with Amadou to the incredibly beautiful summer palace. She told me how they sat together near some fragrant lemon trees and recited poetry. They were so absorbed in each other that they ignored passers-by and lost track of the time. Simone's memories were so vivid and enthralling that I couldn't help wondering if I'd ever experience anything close to what they did. The more I wondered, the sadder I became. I'm about the same age as Simone when she went to Paris and met Amadou. What is there in my life? A room at my father's place, and two parents who don't care for each other."

Sara could tell Pastel was getting worked up again. She drew close and hugged her. "I agree that you've gotten a late start on the life you'd like to live, but you took an important first step by deciding to be a writer. That required a great deal of courage."

"And you've got two people here who care deeply for you," Simone added.

Sara stared at Pastel for a moment without saying anything. "I'm having some struggles of my own right now," she finally admitted. "See that tent over there. I got here early and decided to have my fortune told. You'll never guess what the fortune teller told me."

"I haven't a clue," Pastel replied. "I'd be afraid to have my fortune told."

"She said I had come to her because of a man."

"Of course you did," Simone said with an indulgent smile. "You're a woman."

"I know it was predictable, but then she told me there can be no peace where there is desire. Does that mean I must choose between peace and desire?"

"Could it have been a warning to avoid wanting something too much?" Pastel asked.

"Do you think peace is more important than desire?" Sara responded.

"Be careful about artificial dichotomies," Simone advised in her best professorial voice. "It could mean nothing more than this: In order to achieve peace, you first must satisfy your desire, whatever that might be."

"I like Simone's interpretation better than mine," Pastel interjected.

"So, Serenity Castle of Charlottesville, Virginia," Simone began, "what do you desire and what would it take to satisfy that desire?"

Sara's first thought involved Trevor, but she gave Simone another answer. "I'd like to revive my pursuit of art."

"That doesn't sound like desire to me," Simone countered. "It sounds like a default option."

Sara quickly changed the subject by insisting that they needed to get on the road. The ensuing drive to Seville went much like the trip to Granada. Pastel continued asking Simone questions about her life, but instead of eavesdropping as she had done earlier, Sara kept thinking about what the fortune teller said. Could history be repeating itself? Was it possible that she now was facing the same choice she once faced when she fell in love with David: pursue an art career or nurture a new relationship? The question was unsettling.

At this point Sara's practical side took over. "I don't even know if Trevor is interested in me romantically," she acknowledged. "I'm also unsure that I've dealt fully with David's death. Who knows how Marie would react to my having a new relationship? If I decide to pursue art again and it doesn't work out, at least no one gets hurt."

"No one except yourself," Simone added.

Suddenly Sara noticed a sign that indicated Seville was less than a hundred kilometers away. No arrangements had been made for a place to spend the night. Sara asked Pastel to use her cell phone to locate a hotel, preferably one in the old section of Seville.

Pastel found a historic hotel in the Jewish quarter that boasted having a Michelin two-star restaurant as well as a popular piano bar. Sara and Simone agreed the place sounded intriguing. Pastel volunteered to sleep on a couch so that only one double room would be required, but Simone wanted her own room, explaining that she frequently had trouble sleeping and often needed to get up and read for a while. Pastel called the hotel and reserved two rooms.

By the time Sara negotiated Seville traffic and reached the hotel, no one wished to try out the piano bar or the highly rated restaurant. All Sara and Pastel wanted was to order room service and take a relaxing bath. They planned to meet Simone for breakfast in the morning and complete their pilgrimage to Lisbon. Before dropping off Simone at her room, Sara told her to call if she needed assistance during the night.

When Sara and Pastel reached their room, they found it to be exquisite. The antique furnishings could have graced an aristocrat's mansion. Two large windows overlooked a lovely courtyard bursting with fragrant flowers and centered by a bubbling fountain. The bathroom was as large as most hotel rooms. Ceiling fans provided a cooling breeze that permitted the windows to remain open so that the scents of jasmine and orange blossoms from the courtyard could fill the room.

After the orders for room service were placed, Sara asked Pastel if she planned on turning her notes on Simone's life into an article or a book.

"I've only scratched the surface of a very complex and compelling individual," she responded. "Simone said something very intriguing when we were in the summer palace's garden. I half expected her to repeat it when you told us about what the fortune teller had said."

"By all means, tell me."

"I asked Simone whether she would have married Amadou if he had proposed to her. She responded that desire and marriage are incompatible. I asked for an explanation, and she observed that marriage turns a couple into an economic unit committed more to the efficient management of a household than emotional support and passion."

CHAPTER 16

Sara awoke once again with her mind locked in high gear. The people she met on the cruise had introduced her to thoughts and perspectives that caught her off-guard. Not since David died had she been compelled to confront dormant aspects of her being. The most recent cause for overnight restlessness was Simone's remark to Pastel about marriage. Cursed with a tendency to personalize such comments, Sara wondered if her marriage had evolved from enthrallment to economics.

Gazing out the window at the courtyard, Sara was pleased to see so much color. A delicate, refreshing breeze wafted across her face. Pastel briefly stirred, then turned away to resume sleeping. Sara reached over to gently shake Pastel and inform her the time had come to get up. Next, she called Simone to make sure her friend was all right. Simone sounded cheery and reported that her appetite had returned. They agreed to meet for breakfast in forty-five minutes.

When the three travelers were seated in the restaurant, Simone inquired about the upcoming trip to Lisbon. Sara estimated it would take two and a half hours to reach Albufeira on the Portuguese coast and another two and a half hours to get to their destination. Simone was worried about the news that parts of Portugal flooded recently during Cyclone Danielle, and she expressed concern that their travel might be interrupted. Pastel immediately grabbed her cell phone to check. A few moments later she reported that parts of Lisbon and Setubal had experienced wind damage and minor flooding, but the roads remained open in most places. The worst flooding had occurred in the mountains east of Lisbon.

The buffet-style breakfast was sumptuous. Pastel and Sara returned to the table, their plates laden with fruit, cheese, and sliced meat. Simone surprised her companions by choosing an omelet filled with Portuguese sausage and a plate of smoked fish. When Sara and Pastel commented on the size of her breakfast, Simone claimed she needed energy for Lisbon.

Mystified, Sara asked, "Is there something you're not telling us about Lisbon?"

"My dear, there is always something I'm not telling you. Over the years, I've learned that the less I say, the less trouble I get into."

Simone went on to relate a humorous story about one of her undergraduate students, a white guy from Alabama. While lecturing on African literature, she referred to the negritude movement in Francophone Africa. The naive young man believed that negritude was a racist term, equivalent to the "n" word and a derogatory reference to blacks with an attitude.

"The kid was all set to report me to the dean," Simone chuckled, "which could have hurt my chances for promotion. His father happened to be a major donor to the university. I could tell that the young man relished the prospect of reporting a black professor for making a racist remark. I tried to explain to him that negritude was the antithesis of a racist comment, since it referred to a vibrant movement by black Africans to cultivate their own, unique culture."

"Did you ever get through to him?" Pastel asked.

"Not at all. He dropped the class. Just another example of the innocent maligned by the ignorant."

After breakfast the women retrieved their overnight bags and checked out. Sara expressed a desire to return to the hotel one day when she could appreciate all it had to offer. Simone responded by suggesting she consider bringing a male companion on her next visit.

The travelers agreed that the September sunshine and pleasant temperature made for ideal driving conditions. Once again Sara drove while Pastel continued asking Simone about her life. On occasion, Pastel switched from queries about academic experiences to more personal questions, but it became obvious that Simone's academic life was her life, at least after she left Amadou in Paris to work on her doctoral dissertation back home. Sara asked Simone a question about her plans for Lisbon, but just like her earlier attempt at breakfast, the question went unanswered.

After an hour or so of driving, the road began to afford views of the coastline. At one point, Pastel spotted a salt pond with a flamboyance of flamingos enjoying themselves. Several medium-sized resort areas were passed on the way to Albufeira. Rather than stopping in Albufeira for lunch, the women decided to press on to Lisbon. Sara eventually stopped for gas, restroom visits, and light snacks.

Just before one o'clock, Pastel's cell phone buzzed. Alarmed, she picked up the phone. Her father was on the line. From what Sara could gather, Brendan Greene might have contracted COVID because Pastel chastised him for not getting a second booster shot before they left the United States.

Once the call ended, Sara asked, "Is your father okay?"

"He's uncertain if he has the virus, but he opted not to be tested anyway. Dad wants to be able to leave the ship in Lisbon and not face the possibility of having to quarantine. He canceled our flight home and booked a hotel for several days, just in case his condition worsens. I was advised to make my own hotel arrangements. If it turns out he does have COVID, he didn't want me exposed to it."

Simone asked if Pastel was concerned about her father. She replied that he received the original vaccination and a booster, so if he did catch COVID, his case shouldn't be too serious. "Besides," she added, "he'll relish a few days of solitude to think about his next book."

"You needn't worry about a place to sleep," Simone interjected. "I've made arrangements for the three of us to stay in a lovely boutique hotel in one of Lisbon's historic districts. I took the liberty of having you and Sara share a room."

"That was very thoughtful," Pastel replied," especially since I no longer have a ticket to fly home. Do you have something exciting planned?"

"I wouldn't use the word exciting, but I did hope we could

have a farewell dinner tomorrow night before we go our separate ways. I made reservations at a favorite restaurant of mine."

"I can't think of anything I'd rather do or two people I'd rather do it with," Sara responded enthusiastically.

"Not even Trevor?" Pastel asked.

"Not even Trevor."

A few minutes later Sara's cell phone jingled. She picked up the phone with one hand while the other hand steered the SUV to the roadside. All the color drained from Sara's face as she took the call. Under her breath, she whispered, "I hope nothing's happened to Marie and Marcus."

"Or Randy," Pastel added.

Sara didn't even say hello. "Is everything all right, Marie? It must be early morning at home."

There was no panic in Marie's voice, but definitely concern. She told her mother that Randy had called and mentioned having lunch with Sara in Barcelona. He also noted that Sara hadn't purchased a return ticket. "I hope you're not planning on doing anything foolish," Marie advised.

"I can assure you I do not plan on doing anything foolish, my dear, but perhaps something a bit impractical. Let's leave it at that, if you don't mind."

"You haven't met a man, have you?"

"I've met quite a few men."

"Don't be coy, Mom. You know what I mean."

"Listen, Marie, you have plenty to deal with now that you're moving. Don't worry about me. It might surprise you to know that I'm an adult. I've met some delightful individuals on my cruise. It's high time I rejoined the world of the living."

"When were you intending to come home?"

"I haven't decided yet, Marie."

"This isn't like you, Mom."

"I appreciate your saying that. It's exactly what I needed to hear."

"You'll be home for the holidays, won't you?"

"Listen, my love, I'm on my way to Lisbon at the moment. When I figure out my plans, you'll be the first to know." Sara ended the call knowing that Marie had additional questions to ask.

"Your daughter's worried about you, isn't she?" Pastel asked.

"She's definitely worried, but I'm not sure what she's worried about. Marie thrives on predictability, especially where I'm concerned. It'll be good for her to have a little uncertainty in her life."

Not much more was said until the travelers reached the outskirts of Lisbon. Sara requested directions to the hotel Simone had booked.

"I recommend turning in the SUV and taking a taxi to the Hotel Pessoa," Simone advised. "The Alfama district where we're staying is a maze of steep and narrow streets and alleys. It's the oldest neighborhood in Lisbon. Driving can be treacherous and parking is scarce."

Pastel picked up her cell phone and located the rental agency. It was not far from the highway, and Sara was able to drive there without much difficulty. The helpful rental agent called a taxi for his clients.

On the way to the hotel, Simone explained that it was named for Fernando Pessoa, one of Portugal's best-known writers and a recipient of the Nobel Prize in Literature. She went on to admit that his best-known work, The Book of Disquiet, was probably the most difficult book she'd ever read. Pessoa referred to his masterpiece as a "factless autobiography." Pastel expressed an interest in reading it, though Simone warned her to wait a while.

The Hotel Pessoa was tucked away on a cobblestone side street that looked more like an alley. The antiquated building was adorned with Lisbon's famous azulejos tiles. Sara figured it must once have been a wealthy family's home. After checking in, Pastel suggested that the three meet at six o'clock and find a nearby restaurant. Simone apologized, saying she needed to take care of a few things that evening. Sara suspected, however, that her friend simply was exhausted from two days on the road and probably in considerable pain. Before parting, arrangements were made to meet in the morning for breakfast before heading to the port to collect their luggage from the ship.

Sara and Pastel asked the desk clerk for dinner suggestions.

All of his recommendations were within walking distance, but he warned that several places to eat were located at the bottom of the hill. If they chose one of these restaurants, he advised them to take the number twenty-eight tram back to the hotel, as the walk could be very challenging, especially at night after a bottle of delicious Portuguese wine.

Sara and Pastel found their room pleasant, but not as spacious or charming as their accommodations in Seville. The windows looked out on the wall of an adjacent building. Pastel wondered how often Simone had stayed in the Hotel Pessoa and whether these occasions had been with Amadou. Sara took a few photographs of the room in case she decided to paint it one day.

"Just like Van Gogh did?" Pastel asked.

"Yes, but fortunately there's more to work with here."

Pastel suggested Sara shower first so she could check her text messages. When Sara returned from the bathroom, Pastel was aglow.

"Guess who texted me?"

"Damian."

"Really, Sara? It was your son. He's looking forward to seeing me at Thanksgiving."

"If he's serious about coming to Charlottesville for Thanksgiving, I'd better plan to be back home by then," Sara said with a wink.

While Pastel showered, Sara went on-line to review the menus of the restaurants recommended by the desk clerk. The most intriguing dinner choices belonged to the Pescador e Enologo, which Sara guessed meant the fisherman and the winemaker. When she showed the menu to Pastel, her young friend agreed. Since the desk clerk had characterized all his recommendations as "casual chic" establishments, the two women decided to wear slacks and short-sleeved pullovers.

In the hotel lobby Pastel requested directions to the restaurant. After praising her choice, the desk clerk told her to descend to the bottom of the hill and turn right. As they negotiated the winding, uneven sidewalks of the Alfama, both women were glad they left their high heels on the ship.

The Pescador e Enologo was bustling with diners when Sara

and Pastel arrived. Both commented on the appealing ambience. Pastel reminded me of restaurants in New York City's Little Italy. Sara liked the abundance of candles and the soft sounds of recorded jazz. Learning that no tables were available until much later, the women opted to sit at the bar.

The only adjoining seats that were unoccupied were located at the far end of the bar. Sara took the last seat and Pastel the one on her left. She purposely chose the last seat when she noticed that Pastel would be seated next to an attractive man with a mop of uncombed black hair and a shadow of beard. Sara thought he bore a striking resemblance to a young George Harrison.

After ordering two glasses of a red blend from the Alentejo region that the bartender recommended, the women revisited the extensive menu and decided on the braised pork and clams. When the wine arrived, they toasted their friendship. Pastel then turned and looked directly at Sara.

"I'd like to know what you've decided about pursuing your dream. Simone believes it's imperative that you reconnect with your youthful quest to become an artist. She admitted to me that the only reason her cancer has been bearable is because she achieved her dream of becoming a professor."

Sara wasn't sure she wanted to address such a serious topic over dinner, but she also recognized it was unwise to keep avoiding the subject. "As long as you bring it up, I'll be honest with you. I'm worried that it's too late for me to start painting again. I'm not as flexible as I once was and my eyesight is declining as well as my stamina."

"Why were you once consumed by the desire to become an artist?"

Sara mulled over Pastel's question and requested another glass of wine. "I've always been a visual person. When I think, I typically think in images that I believe are unique to me. It may sound silly to you, but I wanted to paint those unique images. I felt I had a gift."

"That doesn't sound silly at all. What we create is the truest expression of who we are."

The voice that Sara heard was not Pastel's. It came from the young man sitting next to her. She quickly swiveled on her bar stool and looked at Pastel's neighbor. "Are you an artist?" Pastel asked.

"I apologize for eavesdropping," the man replied, "but your friend was speaking my language, and I don't mean Portuguese. Let me say that I am learning to be an artist."

"You're an art student?"

"Jose Silva at your service. And you are?"

"Pastel Greene, fledgling writer."

Jose smiled.

"I know, it's my name. My mother is an artist."

"That is not why I smile. I would have guessed your mother was a baker. In Portuguese, Pastel means pastry."

Sara and Pastel laughed out loud. Then Pastel said, "Let me introduce my friend. This is Serenity Castle, but everyone calls her Sara."

"I prefer Serenity. What a charming name," Jose responded.

Dinner lasted much longer than either woman expected. They both found Jose to be a fascinating companion. He spoke about what it was like to study painting at the Faculdade de Belas-Artes da Universidade de Lisboa. Students came from all over the world to take courses there. Jose offered to take Sara with him if she wished to see what classes were like. Sara wrote down his cell phone number and promised to consider the offer.

Jose spent considerable time quizzing Pastel about her plans to become a writer. She told him of her desire to paint pictures with words, word-pictures that would move people to reconsider their assumptions about the world in which they live.

When her turn came, Pastel questioned Jose's reasons for studying art. His response impressed her. "I paint to release feelings within me that I cannot express in words."

The three consumed a great deal of wine and lost all track of time. Jose finally checked his cell phone and discovered it was almost midnight. He acknowledged that making his nine o'clock class in the morning would be a challenge, then asked Pastel and Sara if they had far to go. When they mentioned the Hotel Pessoa, he praised their choice, saying it was the perfect spot for a painter and a writer. For the first time in many years, someone referred to Sara as a painter. She liked the sound of it.

Jose pointed out that the tram would not be running at that late hour. He offered to walk his new friends back to the hotel, and they accepted. The three of them, unsteady from so much wine, held hands as they navigated the meandering streets up the hill. Jose suggested that Sara and Pastel find time to visit the Castelo de Sao Jorge, a few meters further up the hill from the hotel. The view of Lisbon was breathtaking, he noted.

When the group reached the hotel, Jose hugged Sara and Pastel and told them he hoped their paths would cross again. Back in the room, Pastel asked Sara if she intended to visit art classes with Jose.

"Tomorrow, we need to see what Simone has in mind for our farewell dinner. I just might have to buy a new dress for such a special occasion. After tomorrow, however, I think both of us should attend classes with Jose."

CHAPTER 17

TUESDAY, SEPTEMBER 27, 2022

Sara didn't know if she heard the alarm go off and drifted back to sleep or never heard it in the first place. Regardless, Simone and Pastel had already been served breakfast when she finally arrived at the hotel dining room looking somewhat hung over from the night before. Pastel recommended the pastel de nata, an egg tart enjoyed by many Portuguese. Simone ate small bites from a cheese and ham sandwich. Sara ordered the egg tart and a double espresso.

"I understand you and Pastel closed down the bar last night," Simone said in a tone of mock disapproval.

"We met a delightful art student named Jose Silva. He even invited me to visit his art classes," Sara replied.

"I hope you accepted his invitation. Lisbon would be a perfect place for you to resume your art studies."

The three chatted about the farewell dinner, agreeing that it was an occasion worthy of glamour. Simone planned to wear a "stylishly sedate dress befitting my age". Sara and Pastel responded that they might have to go shopping for something appropriately classy. Simone requested that her friends collect her small carry-on suitcase when they went to the ship terminal to get their own luggage. She also asked that they be ready to leave the hotel for dinner at eight o'clock and mentioned they'd be going to a fado restaurant.

During the taxi ride to the port, Sara and Pastel speculated about what Simone might have in mind for the farewell dinner. Despite all of Pastel's personal questions for Simone during the drive to Lisbon, there was much about the woman that remained a mystery. Sara, for instance, wondered what combination of personal strengths enabled Simone to overcome parental abandonment, spousal abuse, lost love, and racial and gender discrimination on her way to becoming an internationally esteemed scholar.

By the time the taxi reached the port-side waiting area where passengers claimed their luggage, it was after ten. Pastel received a text message from her father indicating that he had disembarked and was on his way to a hotel. He didn't mention how he was feeling, so Pastel planned to contact him later. Sara had no problem locating their suitcases because Trevor was standing beside them. So glad she was to see him that she rushed over and delivered a hug.

Trevor asked about the drive to Lisbon and what Sara and Pastel planned to do for the day. Both spoke at the same time about needing to do some serious shopping for Simone's farewell dinner.

"Have you decided to stay in Lisbon for a while?" Trevor asked.

Pastel responded first. "I'll be here as long as my father wants to stay." Nothing was said about the possibility Brendan Greene had contracted COVID.

Trevor looked expectantly at Sara. She sensed what was on his mind. "There's no reason for me to rush back to Virginia," she replied. "I have learned there's a well-known art program at the University of Lisbon. I might wander over to campus and see what they offer for fifty-five-year-old beginners."

"You're hardly a novice," Pastel insisted.

"As it turns out," Trevor began, "I also have no reason to return immediately to the United States. Would you consider me too presumptuous if I remained in Lisbon for a few days so we could do some sightseeing together?"

Sara blushed bright crimson. "What a lovely idea. Pastel and I are staying at the Hotel Pessoa in the Alfama district."

"You've got my cell phone number, and I have yours," Trevor replied. "I know you're tied up tonight. Why don't I contact you tomorrow and we can discuss possibilities. In the meantime, I need to locate a place to stay."

Sara considered recommending the Hotel Pessoa, but decided it would be better to allow things to move along more slowly.

Trevor helped Sara and Pastel shift the suitcases to the street and then hailed a taxi for them. Once they were settled in the vehicle, he waved goodbye and returned to retrieve his own luggage.

On the way back to the hotel, Sara asked Pastel to think about a toast for Simone's farewell dinner. Then she searched on her cell phone for dress shops around the Alfama district. Several interesting stores popped up, including one that advertised ensembles for the "fadista" in every woman. "That sounds like the place to go," Sara announced. "Simone is planning on having our dinner at a fado restaurant."

Once the suitcases were brought by the doorman to their room, Sara and Pastel went to Simone's room with her carry-on suitcase. They knocked on the door, but no one answered. Pastel asked a maid to open Simone's door and deposit the suitcase. Glancing inside, Sara was surprised to see a bottle of whiskey on Simone's dressing table. Had the maid not been present, she would have liked to snoop around for a moment.

Back in the hotel lobby, the two women asked for directions to the "fadista" dress shop. The desk clerk recommended taking the tram twenty-eight. After a brief wait, the colorful yellow and white tram arrived, packed with an assortment of humanity including several construction workers, an elderly couple holding on for dear life when the tram's brakes were applied, three college-age males on their cell phones, and a large group of Asian tourists who continuously snapped photographs. Pastel took a cell phone shot of the tram and sent it to Sara's cell phone in case she wanted to paint it one day.

Tram twenty-eight threaded its way through the Alfama, past fado bars, bistros, small shops, and churches. Eventually it reached the Rua Augusta and a large commercial area. According to Pastel's cell phone, the dress shop was several blocks from the tram stop, so the two women hopped off the tram and began walking.

Sara thought of the days when David was her traveling companion. He always made sure to find a map of the area they planned to visit because he couldn't bring himself to trust directions on his cell phone. David prided himself on being able to picture where he and Sara were going well before they actually went there. In that sense, and that sense only, he was a visual thinker like Sara. What would Pastel and the rest of her generation ever do, Sara wondered, if their cell phones failed to function?

In the distance Sara spotted a large arch leading to an enormous plaza bordered on three sides by offices and shops. Pastel informed her that they needed to turn right before entering the plaza. A short walk brought them to a stately establishment named the Palace of Dresses. Surveying the impressive three-story art deco building, Sara told Pastel, "This won't be cheap."

"We can look for another place if you'd like," Pastel offered.

"I wouldn't think of it. Simone deserves the best."

The pair were greeted at the door by a lovely dark-haired, middle-aged woman who addressed them in impeccable English. Were they just browsing or searching for something in particular? she asked. Sara explained the occasion they would be attending that evening and their desire "to glow, but not too brightly."

"My name is Maria Elena," the woman said. "If you'll follow me, I believe we can find the perfect dress for each of you."

Using the antique elevator, the trio went to the second floor where dozens of dresses were displayed, some in clever tableaux made to resemble fancy restaurants and dance venues, others on individual mannequins lined up along the aisles. After strolling around for several minutes, Sara found a manakin wearing a sleeveless, knee-length dress that flared at the bottom. When she tried on the dress, Pastel declared that she looked stunning and snapped her picture.

Maria Elena concurred, adding, "The decolletage is perfect for a woman, shall I guess in her early forties, with a very attractive figure. She has no need to boast or show off. She is her own woman."

"You've got that right," Pastel added.

Sara smiled. "Perhaps you need glasses, Maria Elena. I am fifty-five."

"Your age is well-concealed. I can only hope to be so fortunate." Turning to Pastel, the sales woman said, "How about you, young lady? Your coloring is different from your mother's. Perhaps something in a lighter shade of blue or maybe pink?"

"Sara is not my mother, though she would have made a wonderful one. I agree with you about my coloring. My name, after all, is Pastel."

"Like Portuguese pastry."

"You're not the first person to point that out."

"Please do not be offended."

As Maria Elena and Pastel considered different dress styles, Sara drifted into thoughts about what men Pastel's age found attractive in women. Her opinion was they were uninterested in haute couture. Slim jeans and snug-fitting tops seemed to be the preferred garments.

Pastel gravitated to several mannequins wearing pleated dresses that rose a few inches above the knee and had a higher neckline than the dress Sara chose. After trying on several dresses, Pastel selected a light green one with short sleeves. She asked Sara to take a picture with her cell phone.

Pastel offered to pay for her dress, but Sara insisted on covering the cost of both. "My Marie insisted on picking out her own clothes. She never would choose such a stylish dress. I'm delighted to see you appreciate tasteful fashions."

Both Pastel and Sara complained of being hungry as they left the Palace of Dresses. Near the Rua Augusta, they found a quaint bistro with an adjacent courtyard and requested to be seated near the courtyard fountain. Sara ordered a bowl of fish stew and cornbread. Pastel opted for sausage and kale soup and a cup of rice pudding. Knowing there would be lots of drinking at Simone's farewell dinner, they requested espresso instead of wine.

As the women waited for their food, the conversation somehow turned to mothers. Pastel expressed regrets that she and her mother did not enjoy a closer relationship. Whenever the two of them got together, Karen found a way to make Pastel feel inadequate. Sara admitted that she had difficulty relating to her mother during her teenage years because Gwen spent most of the time protesting something. Gwen wanted Sara to join her at rallies and marches for various causes, but all Sara desired was to work on her art projects and listen to music. Only when her mother developed

Alzheimer's disease and came to live with Sara did the two draw closer. Sara did not mention her fear of developing the disease that took her mother's life.

When lunch was over, Sara and Pastel caught the tram twenty-eight back to the hotel. It was almost four o'clock. Pastel went to a sitting area off the lobby to work on her toast for Simone. Sara planned a leisurely soak in the bathtub followed by a short nap. Before she got on the elevator, the desk clerk handed her a message. Trevor said he looked forward to seeing Lisbon with her over the coming days and left the name of his hotel.

Once in the room, Sara quickly removed her sweaty clothes and filled the tub. Much was on her mind as she eased into the lukewarm water. What will Simone do after this evening's farewell dinner? Will she want to keep in touch? And how about Pastel? Would she return to New York with her father and possibly abandon her plans? Sara wanted to continue encouraging Pastel to pursue a writing career. Then there was Trevor. Has enough time passed since David's death for her to explore a new relationship?

That last question caused Sara to revisit her original intentions for the second honeymoon. She initially looked forward to visualizing special moments with David during their original honeymoon. Now it seemed as if those efforts to stimulate fond memories had not always turned out as she had hoped.

The cumulative impact of confronting such a host of concerns frustrated Sara, not only spoiling her bath, but preventing her from enjoying a restful nap. Her mind was too full of questions without definitive answers. Sara's practical nature demanded clarity. Ambiguity, unfortunately, appeared to be the order of the day.

Sara considered calling Marie or Randy in hopes of discussing her quandaries with an individual who knew her well, but she was hesitant to risk alarming them. It wasn't as though she was teetering on the brink of a breakdown. If only there was a prescription of some kind for clarity. With several hours to go until Simone's retirement dinner, Sara decided to call room service and request a bottle of white Burgundy.

Two glasses of wine enabled Sara to relax enough to put matters into proper perspective. She was embarking on a new chapter in her life. That meant confronting the unknown. Ambiguity was to be expected. What was called for now was patience. Perhaps she might even learn to enjoy the lack of clarity in her life.

Sara's self-talk prompted her to picture herself in her high school cheerleader's uniform yelling encouragement as she reveled in her current state of uncertainty. "Two, four, six, eight, isn't ambiguity great!" For five minutes she couldn't stop laughing at the image.

Simone broke the spell when she called to make sure Sara and Pastel would be ready to depart at eight. A limousine had been ordered to take the three women to Amalia's, a well- known Alfama fado restaurant. Sara guaranteed that she and Pastel would not keep their friend waiting. No sooner had Sara ended the call than Pastel entered the room looking pleased. She liked her toast for Simone's farewell dinner and was anxious to bathe and get dressed.

A few minutes before eight, the three women met at the third-floor elevator. Upon exiting to the lobby, they were greeted by whistles of approval from the desk clerk and bellhop. Guests just arriving at the hotel stopped to admire the trio. Several women asked where they got their dresses, and a young man sitting by himself stood up and offered his services as an escort. An older gentleman with a well-trimmed white beard asked the desk clerk who the fancy ladies were.

Sara and Pastel complimented Simone on how vibrant she looked in her sequined black sheath. The tassels around the hem swished from side to side as she moved. A black shawl was draped over her shoulders. Sara thought she resembled a torch singer from a thirties' movie.

The limousine arrived precisely at eight, and the tuxedoed driver bowed to the trio and escorted them to the vehicle. Once everyone was seated and buckled in, the driver introduced himself and confirmed that they were bound for Amalia's.

"You have chosen a good evening to visit Amalia's," he continued. "There will be fewer young people than on weekends and more well-to-do customers. The fado music also will be more authentic than on Fridays and Saturdays."

Simone turned to Pastel and whispered that she was sorry to hear about the lack of young people. Pastel smiled and responded that young people generally bored her.

The trip to Amalia's only took ten minutes. Sara wished they could have ridden around Lisbon for a bit longer in the luxurious limousine before going to Amalia's. She made a mental note to suggest such an excursion to Trevor. Lisbon at night was certain to be enchanting.

The three women sauntered into Amalia's arm-in-arm, like celebrities who were life-long friends. A portly, middle-aged man in a black tuxedo with a black shirt recognized Simone and kissed her hand. She introduced Domingo to Sara and Pastel as he guided them to a table near the rear of the restaurant and close to a raised platform that served as a stage. Once he assisted each guest in getting seated, Domingo signaled a waiter and departed.

"Are you and Domingo old friends?" Pastel asked Simone.

"We are new friends, my dear, but his father was an old friend." Simone's eyes sparkled when she said this.

Sara did a quick scan of the restaurant. Her intention was to capture enough of the setting to be able to visualize and then sketch it tomorrow and perhaps paint it later on. As a back-up, she also asked Pastel to take a cell phone photo.

The main dining area consisted of around thirty tables of various sizes, half of which were occupied, mostly by couples she estimated were in their fifties and sixties. Each table contained a large candle that complimented the dim overhead lighting. The place reminded Sara of Caravaggio paintings with their alternating patterns of darkness and light. This effect, which her college art instructor referred to as chiaroscuro, caused Sara to think of her own life, a life that vacillated between murky periods and luminous times.

The restaurant walls were adorned with black and white photographs of fadistas who once performed at Amalia's. Blue azulejos tiles surrounded the doorways and archways. Well-worn wooden floors added to the warmth of the dining area. Sara decided the setting was perfect for a melancholic farewell dinner.

The waiter arrived and asked the women if they wished to order drinks before dinner. He added that a fado singer was scheduled to perform her first set at nine o'clock. Simone requested a vermouth aperitif. Pastel and Sara asked for Cosmopolitans.

"For once I feel like an actual adult," Pastel declared.

"I wouldn't mind being a kid again," Sara responded.

After the drinks arrived, Sara asked Simone if it had been hard to retire.

"I was not prepared to suddenly be irrelevant," Simone answered. "If my health had allowed it, I planned to teach until I reached seventy-five, then write a book about my life. Now I gladly leave Pastel in charge of compiling my earthly odyssey. I made her promise to write an honest account, not a fluff piece."

"Perhaps if I can resurrect my painting skills, I could paint a portrait of you," Sara added.

"Did you know," Pastel began, "that Simone took the money from the sale of her home and created an endowed chair for a professor of African literature? She told me that few literature programs pay sufficient attention to the work coming out of Africa."

"Amadou would have loved what you did."

"He should," Simone replied. "The chair is endowed in his name."

Pastel tapped on her water glass with a fork. "I would like to offer a toast to our lovely friend. Few people in this world can truly say that they lived the life that they chose. Our Simone is one of them. But that's not all. In living the life that she chose, she also enriched the lives of countless others, including Sara and myself. Simone is proof that joy and sadness must coexist for life to be meaningful and lived to the fullest."

Sara added, "If life was a flavor, it would be bittersweet."

Simone grabbed a napkin to dry her eyes.

Pastel picked up her Cosmopolitan and said, "Please raise your glass to honor a remarkable individual."

Sara nodded her approval to Pastel as she toasted.

"It's a good thing my skin is black," Simone said, "so you can't see me blushing." Her companions laughed so loudly at the remark that people seated at neighboring tables turned to see what was so funny.

When the waiter returned to take dinner orders, all three women expressed the desire for a second round of drinks first. "We're in no hurry for this evening to end," Pastel told him.

"I'd be interested in hearing your views on American society,"

Sara said to Simone.

"I wish I could be more optimistic, but I believe our current divisions will only grow wider. There is little interest, it seems, in forging a common culture. Instead, many choose what they watch, who they listen to, and what they read based on their pre-existing biases. In other words, they purposely seek only to confirm, not question, what they believe. American society has become a hodgepodge of closed-minded cults."

"That's a buzz-kill," Pastel declared. "Is there no hope that things will change?"

"Things won't change until people learn to value what they share in common more than what divides them."

The second round of drinks arrived, and the three women nursed them as they discussed hopes and fears for the world. Pastel finally suggested changing topics. Simone asked Sara if she had thought any more about pursuing her interest in art. Sara discussed meeting Jose Silva and wanting to learn more about his art curriculum at the University of Lisbon.

The waiter returned and advised the women to put in their dinner orders before the fado performance began. Sara inquired about the restaurant's specialty dishes, and he singled out octopus with olive oil and potatoes, duck rice with chorizo, and arroz de marisco (seafood rice). Simone selected the arroz de marisco, while Sara and Pastel opted for the duck rice with chorizo.

No sooner had the orders been placed than Domingo walked to the stage to introduce the evening's performer. Sara was surprised to discover that every table was now occupied. As Domingo addressed the audience in Portuguese, several musicians joined him on stage. The overhead lights were turned down even more, and a single soft spotlight was focused on the emcee. Eventually switching to English, Domingo welcomed visitors to Lisbon and acknowledged his great honor to introduce Luisa Gonsalves.

The spotlight shifted to the left and followed the fadista as she slowly walked on stage. Sara commented that she wore a black shawl similar to Simone's. The three women agreed that Luisa was striking. Her long black hair was parted down the middle, framing a chalk-white face with high cheekbones and haunting dark eyes. Other than her face and hands, every part of Luisa was covered in black. Simone guessed she was in her mid-fifties and no stranger to life's disappointments.

Initially Luisa turned her back to the audience in order to acknowledge her musicians: a balding guitarist who appeared incapable of smiling, a young blond woman on viola, a tall, gaunt, black man on bass, and a gray-haired pianist with a streak of white in her shoulder-length hair. Suddenly, without notice, Luisa turned toward the audience and began singing, her deep, resonant voice lingering on each word. Only the guitarist accompanied her soulful singing.

Domingo came over to the three women and whispered that Luisa's signature song was entitled "Talvez se chame saudade." The translation, he added, could be found on-line.

Pastel immediately reached for her cell phone to check and reported that the song's title in English was "Maybe It's Called Nostalgia." She passed around her cell phone so Sara and Simone could read the lyrics. Simone's eyes moistened as she read the opening lines:

"This sweet remembrance that bitterly invades me, maybe it doesn't have a name, maybe it's called nostalgia."

By the time Luisa finished her opening number, Sara felt in a trance. She somehow managed to miss both David and Trevor. They would have liked each other she believed. When Luisa began her next song, Sara visualized David meeting Trevor on the cruise. Is it possible, she wondered, to be nostalgic about what could have been as well as what was?

"Are you still with us, my dear?" Simone whispered to Sara.

"I apologize. The strangest sensation came over me just now. Must have been the second Cosmopolitan."

"Don't be so sure. Fado can be hypnotic," Simone asserted. "Luisa's fervent singing sounds like an evocation of Fate herself to take pity on lovers."

Luisa finished her first set at ten o'clock and left the stage along with the musicians. By that time, Sara, Simone, and Pastel had finished their entrees and were enjoying salad along with white Rioja from Spain. Sara once again raised the subject of what Simone planned to do after this evening.

Simone looked away for a moment. The guitarist for some

reason had returned to the stage. Preoccupied with the guitarist, Simone briefly responded to Sara's query. "I've been a planner my entire adult life, but there's no reason now to plan anymore."

In the past Sara would have found such indecisiveness difficult to understand. People needed to plan if they were to accomplish anything worthwhile in life. David exemplified that belief. Now, though, Sara was beginning to appreciate Simone's refusal to look beyond the moment. Wasn't that Sara's thinking when she purposely decided not to purchase a return plane ticket?

Pastel had been quiet for a while. When Sara asked if she was worried about her father, Pastel shook her head and said he'd be fine even if he did contract the virus. Her worries, she acknowledged, had more to do with going back to New York and possibly losing her support network along with her newfound focus on becoming a writer. Pastel looked to Sara, then to Simone.

Simone, however, did not respond to Pastel, but instead announced she needed to visit the restroom. She rose with difficulty, put on the shawl she had earlier removed, and walked toward the rear of the dining area. Sara expressed concern for Simone's condition.

"I hope she's feeling okay. She's not used to drinking so much. Do you think I should go with her?"

"Give her a few minutes," Pastel answered. "Simone dislikes people trying to take care of her. I thought my mother was an independent person, but Simone puts her to shame."

The other musicians joined the guitarist on stage and began chatting with each other. Ten minutes passed, and Sara decided to check on Simone. No sooner had she stood up, however, than Domingo walked on stage and stepped up to the microphone. Sara sat down.

"That was a short break," Pastel commented.

"Honored guests," Domingo began in English, "Amalia's has a very special performer this evening. She is not a newcomer to this restaurant. Forty years ago, she visited Amalia's with a close friend. My father remembered them with fondness. Her friend, sadly, is no longer with us. Dr. Simone Baker understands saudade, the spirit of fado. That spirit also is found in the music Americans call the blues. Please give a warm welcome to Simone Baker."

Sara and Pastel looked at each other in disbelief as they joined the audience in applauding their companion.

Simone did not appear immediately. A minute or two passed, and Sara wondered if Simone changed her mind. Then she remembered Simone's description of her youthful blues performances. True to form, Simone emerged slowly from the shadows and stood before the microphone. Her sequined dress sparkled in the spotlight's beam that showed down on her frail form. She eyed the crowd momentarily, then focused on several women, asking each one, "Miss, do you know the blues?" The first woman did not respond, but the next one offered a wry smile and replied, "O sim, senhora."

Pastel whispered, "She's doing it, Sara. Just like she told us about her teenage gigs in St. Louis."

A shiver passed through Sara's body. Could this really be happening? The woman is dying of cancer.

Simone took a step toward a couple sitting to her left and asked the man, "Does your companion have the blues?" He nodded. "And are you the reason?" Laughter rippled through the audience.

Moving back to the microphone, Simone told the audience that she was very young when she first performed. At the time people questioned what such a young woman knew about the blues.

"Look at me now. No one, I imagine, would doubt that I know the blues." This time there was no laughter. Sara and Pastel wiped their eyes.

"The song I have chosen for this evening is dedicated to an old friend and two new friends." Sara detected a break in Simone's voice when she said "old friend."

Simone turned toward the band and whispered something. Then she placed both hands around the base of the microphone and in a voice both deep and scarred by heartbreak began to sing.

"Don't know why there's no sun up in the sky. Stormy weather. Since my man and I ain't together, it keeps raining all of the time."

Along with the rest of the audience, Sara and Pastel were mesmerized. The band adjusted their loudness so as not to override Simone's voice. There was an intimacy and an authenticity to the performance that rendered Simone's pain and regret palpable.

Sara couldn't help recalling the moment she learned that David had died in an accident.

"And I just can't get my poor self together. Oh, I'm weary all of the time." Simone proceeded slowly, rhythmically, investing each word with feeling.

When Simone reached, "All I do is pray the Lord will let me walk in the sun once more," there wasn't a dry eye in the crowd. Trevor now entered Sara's thoughts. Could he offer her a walk in the sun? Pastel meanwhile took several photos of Simone and then reached over to take Sara's hand in hers.

When the song ended, everyone including the band members stood and clapped. Many yelled "Encore." Simone offered a warm smile, thanked the band, and returned to her table. Looking at her friend, Sara knew she was spent. What hidden reservoir of determination had Simone been able to tap in order to perform? No one other than Sara and Pastel would ever have guessed that over four decades passed since Simone last sang in public or that she was dying of cancer. The blues truly were a part of Simone's being.

For a long time after the performance, audience members stopped by Simone's table to praise her. So, too, did Luisa Gonsalves. She acknowledged that Simone was a true fadista. The waiter brought drinks to the three women from admirers. Sara asked Simone how long ago she had decided to give her performance. She admitted considering it shortly after receiving her diagnosis.

Pastel wondered why, of all the places she and Amadou visited in Europe, did she pick Lisbon for her performance.

"Amadou and I first made love here. We pledged ourselves to each other and promised to marry when I completed my doctorate. It was the first and only time in my life that I felt my soul was not entirely my own."

CHAPTER 18

WEDNESDAY, SEPTEMBER 28, 2022

Sara, Simone, and Pastel did not leave Amalia's until well past midnight. Luisa Gonsalves sang several more sets following Simone's magical performance. At one point, the fadista invited Simone to do another blues number, but Simone declined. Between sets, people stopped at Simone's table to ask about her background and singing career. Domingo wondered if Simone would consider returning to Amalia's for a longer performance. Simone admitted being flattered, but told him she had other plans. No mention was made of her illness.

Given the lateness of the hour and the quantity of alcohol consumed, the three women assisted each other as they left Amalia's and climbed into the taxi that Domingo had ordered. The driver asked his passengers if they had any interest in visiting an after-hours fado bar near the waterfront. The women responded in unison that the only place they wished to visit was their bedroom.

Back at the Hotel Pessoa, the night clerk welcomed the group and asked if they had enjoyed their evening out. Pastel replied that the visit to Amalia's had been "an unexpected enchantment." The clerk seemed puzzled by her reply.

When they reached their adjoining rooms, Sara asked Simone if she required help getting ready for bed. Simone asked her to unzip her dress.

"I hope you're not planning to sneak out of here tomorrow before we can say goodbye," Sara said.

"I can assure you, my friend, that I have no intention of sneaking out."

Sara and Pastel entered their room and helped each other with the zippers on their dresses. "I'm not sure I trust Simone to wait for us in the morning," Pastel mentioned. "I get the impression she hates goodbyes."

"You may be right. I'll set my alarm for seven."

The two women took turns using the bathroom. Sara normally slept in the nude, but tonight she wore a nightgown in deference to Pastel. Pastel donned pajama bottoms with little penguins in various poses and an NYPD tee shirt. Just as they turned out the bedside lights, there was a knock at the door.

Switching on her light, Sara said, "I hope Simone isn't in trouble."

"Make sure it's Simone before you answer it," Pastel advised. "This isn't Charlottesville."

Sara asked who was knocking, and Simone identified herself. Sara opened the door and invited Simone to come in, but she remained in the hallway.

"I didn't mean to disturb you, but I felt bad about not thanking you and Pastel for all you've done for me during this trip. I couldn't have carried out my plan without you, and I wanted you to know how grateful I am."

Simone seemed a bit tipsy as she reached out to steady herself against the wall. Sara could smell alcohol on her breath and thought she might have had a nightcap before going to bed. Still, there was something not quite right about her friend. Her speech, normally precise and clearly delivered, was slightly slurred. Sara reasoned that Simone must be taking drugs for her cancer. With all the alcohol she drank at Amalia's, it was no wonder she seemed a little out of sorts.

"Are you feeling, okay?" Sara asked. "Would you like to sleep with us tonight? I could take the sofa."

"I'm just tired and a little melancholy. Nothing out of the ordinary."

"Let me help you back to your room. You've had a very eventful evening; one I'll remember the rest of my life."

"As will I," Pastel called out from the bed.

Simone insisted no assistance was needed, but Sara wrapped an arm around her friend's tiny waist and escorted her back to her room. As they passed the chest of drawers, Sara noticed the bottle of whiskey was half full. There were several containers of pills next to it, and one container was open. No pills were inside. The label said oxycodone.

"Simone, what have you done?" Sara asked in an alarmed voice.

"No one lives forever, my dear Sara."

Sara called out to Pastel, who by this time was standing in the doorway to her room. She hurried over to Simone's room.

"You're still alive, Simone. Tonight's performance proved that."

"As you know..." Simone's words faded away as she winced, clutched her side, and dropped on the bed.

"She's fading fast, Pastel." By this time Pastel had noticed the pill containers and bottle of scotch. She began to cry.

Simone made a concerted effort to collect herself just long enough to say, "I can die knowing that I've lived the life I chose to live. Not many people can say that, can they?"

Simone's head fell back and her eyes closed. Sara and Pastel placed her head on the pillow and moved her legs so they didn't dangle over the side.

"Shouldn't we notify the desk clerk so he can call for an ambulance?" Pastel sounded panicky.

"This is the way Simone chose to die. She has been in enormous pain with no hope of recovery. She's in a place that is very special to her. I think we should honor her wishes."

Sara knelt beside the bed and spoke softly in Simone's ear. "I know you can still hear me, Simone. Pastel and I won't let you die alone." Sara motioned for Pastel to lie down on Simone's right side. Then she reclined on her left side. Both women nestled closely to their friend. It didn't take long for Simone's breathing to cease.

Sara and Pastel remained beside her for another hour or so before getting up. Sara decided she'd call the front desk in the morning and report that she couldn't reach Simone and was worried about her. Pastel cautioned her not to disturb anything in the room as they left.

"No one must know that we were with Simone just before she died."

Back in their room, Pastel said, "I wonder what Simone's life would have been like if she had known that Amadou was alive."

"She still would have died of pancreatic cancer," Sara replied.

"That's true, but she might have fought harder to live as long as she could if she and Amadou had been together. Maybe he wouldn't have contracted COVID."

"I'm glad she went the way she did, still alert, insightful, able to hold an audience spellbound. I can't imagine anything worse than slowly melting away like the last pitiful particles of dirty snow after a storm."

The two women went to bed, but neither slept. Sara's head was full of practical matters. Would there be an autopsy and a police investigation? Should Simone's body be returned to St. Louis? Did she leave funds to cover her expenses?

Sara arose at seven, dressed quickly, and phoned the desk clerk, asking him to connect her to Simone's room. After letting the phone ring for several minutes, he reported there was no answer. Sara explained that Simone was very ill and asked him to have someone check immediately to see if she was okay. He speculated that Simone could be in the shower and unable to hear the phone, but Sara insisted that someone check on her. The desk clerk reluctantly agreed to do so.

When he arrived, the desk clerk stopped at Sara's room and handed her a letter. It had been left yesterday with instructions to be delivered today. Sara wondered who would have left a letter for her. She and Pastel waited in the hallway as the young man knocked on Simone's door. When no one answered, he opened the door and called out. Then he saw that Simone was still in bed and quickly retreated to the hallway, telling Sara he didn't wish to wake her.

"How do you know she's not unconscious?" Pastel angrily responded.

Sara called out, "Simone, it's Sara. Are you okay?"

No answer.

Sara repeated what she had said.

All three individuals then entered the room, and the desk clerk felt Simone's pulse. He said something in Portuguese and crossed himself. Then he asked Sara and Pastel to leave the room.

"I will call the authorities. We must not touch anything."

Sara was still holding the letter that the desk clerk had handed her. While he placed a call on his cell phone, she returned to the room with Pastel to read the mysterious letter. It was from Simone.

"By the time you read this letter, you will know that I have ended my life. My wish is to have my body cremated and the ashes cast upon the waters of the Tagus." The letter went on to give the name and contact information for Simone's lawyer in St. Louis. She anticipated that the Portuguese authorities would want verification of her suicide and desire to be cremated. Simone authorized the lawyer to transfer funds to cover her cremation.

Two more paragraphs followed these details. The first was intended for Pastel. "My dear Pastel, if I had been blessed with a daughter, I would have wanted her to be exactly like you: inquisitive, resilient, and caring. Should you decide to write about my life, I ask only that you avoid flattery and sentimentality. Truth was always more important to me than blandishment. Most of my papers can be found at the Washington University library." Pastel was sobbing as she finished.

Sara then read the last paragraph. "Remember, my dear Serenity, that art will enrich you, but only the people you care about will sustain you. Do not allow yourself to become enslaved by memories." Sara, too, began to weep.

The two women hugged each other. "You know what last night was?" Pastel cried. "Simone's farewell dinner was also her wake. Wasn't it just like her to attend her own wake?"

Laughter now mixed with tears. Shifting into her practical gear, Sara noted that the contents of Simone's letter needed to be shared with the authorities when they arrived. Then she said, "I've got to call Trevor."

Sara hoped she didn't awaken Trevor or possibly interrupt something pleasurable. Who knows, she thought. He's an attractive widower. Perhaps he met someone last night and she stayed over. Sara tried to remain cavalier about that prospect, but jealousy prevailed.

Trevor answered on the third ring and, recognizing the caller, gaily responded, "Top of the morning to you," in a pretty good Irish brogue.

Sara skipped the normal pleasantries and told Trevor that Simone passed away during the night. "I feel responsible for carrying out her wishes regarding cremation, but I'm clueless about what needs to be done. Pastel and I could really use your support. We're both pretty shaken."

"Regrettably, as you know, I have some experience with a loved one who died abroad. At least Simone wasn't gunned down by a Haitian gang. You're in the Hotel Pessoa, I believe. Give me half an hour."

"I'm so sorry, Trevor. It was wrong of me to ask you for help. I didn't consider your wife's terrible murder. You don't need to be reminded of such a traumatic tragedy."

"Sara, I want to help in any way I can. Have the local authorities arrived?"

"Not as far as I know. Our room was next to Simone's. I'll wait for you in the lobby."

Having overheard the conversation, Pastel said she would remain in the room while Sara went to the lobby. "I'd like to start working on an obituary for Simone," she added.

By the time Trevor arrived, the police had come and were questioning the desk clerk. Simone's body remained on the bed.

Sara hugged Trevor and started crying again. He held her as he expressed his condolences. Then they sat down on a bench in the lobby, and Sara explained what had happened that morning and at the farewell dinner. She did not share any details about Simone's final mortal moments.

Sara informed Trevor about the letter Simone left for Pastel and her. She speculated that her friend had planned her suicide back in St. Louis because she made arrangements for her lawyer to confirm that she committed suicide.

"As you probably can guess," Trevor began, "there is considerable red tape associated with a person's death in another country. The U.S. Bureau of Consular Affairs in Lisbon will need to be informed. They'll issue a Consular Report of Death Abroad. Meanwhile a physician must prepare a statement of death, which then must be registered with the local municipal authority. If the police suspect foul play, they might keep Simone's body pending an autopsy. It doesn't appear, however, that an investigation would be required, since Simone notified a lawyer of her intentions and left a confirming letter with you."

"What about her cremation?" Sara asked.

"Once all the paperwork is completed, a funeral director in Lisbon will need to be contacted. I can help you with that. The funeral director must arrange for the body to be cremated."

Sara looked at Trevor. "It is such a comfort to have you here." She held his hand. "We'd better go to my room and check on Pastel. She took Simone's death pretty hard."

When they reached the room, an older man was next door talking with the police officers. They were speaking in Portuguese, but Sara recognized the word oxycodone. She suspected the man was either the coroner or a physician. Pastel thanked Trevor for coming so quickly and hugged him.

"I called my father to see how he was doing," Pastel announced. "He tested negative for COVID, so he's flying back to New York the day after tomorrow. I told him Simone died last night, and he suspected she killed herself rather than endure more pain. He'd do the same thing if he had incurable cancer."

"Will you accompany your father on the flight home?" Sara asked.

"Part of me would love to hang out in Lisbon for a while longer, but I know it's a struggle for him to travel. I'll do the daughterly thing and go with him. Besides, I've got some homework to attend to. I've decided to apply to a first-rate graduate writing program. I'm considering the University of Iowa and the University of Virginia."

"Simone would be so pleased. If you wind up at UVA, you can live with me," Sara offered. "I'd welcome the company."

"That's quite an incentive for coming to Charlottesville," Pastel replied with a smile.

"If I can get accepted for a graduate degree in UVA's School of Architecture, can I live with you too?" Trevor asked. Sara and Pastel exchanged grins.

The three continued to chat while they waited for the authorities to meet with them. Eventually one of the police officers took statements from Sara and Pastel. They described the farewell dinner at Amalia's and Simone's visit to their room before she went to bed. Sara mentioned that, as far as she knew, Simone had no living relatives. Then she showed him the letter in which Simone asked her to handle the arrangements for cremation. The officer promised to notify Sara as soon as the body was released and the proper paperwork was completed.

With no further business for Sara and Pastel regarding Simone's death, Trevor suggested finding a place to have lunch. Pastel declined, saying she wanted to finish the obituary and email it to the St. Louis Post-Dispatch.

"I have an idea," Sara announced. "Why don't we plan on getting together this evening at Amalia's. We need to celebrate Simone's life." Sara passed a slip of paper to Pastel. "Would you contact Jose Silva and invite him to join the three of us for dinner?" Pastel's eyes lit up.

"I'll make reservations for eight thirty. Trevor, would you mind arranging for a limousine?"

Once the reservations were made and the limousine ordered, Sara and Trevor set off on a walk up to the Castelo de Sao Jorge. Along the way they looked for a place to eat lunch. Sara hadn't eaten since the previous evening and admitted to being famished. As they strolled along the winding road, Trevor checked the day's weather and reported that showers were predicted after eight that evening.

Just before the couple reached the entrance gate to the castle grounds, they spotted an inviting little café tucked away along a side street. During a light lunch of fresh fruit and shrimp salad, Sara and Trevor talked continuously. Their apparent hunger for each other's company far surpassed their desire for alimentary nourishment.

Later when Sara looked back on the lunch, she couldn't believe having expressed her feelings of guilt over David. Certainly, there had to be more upbeat topics to be discussed. Maybe she just needed to put the past behind her one final time. Whatever the reason, she confided her original intention to rekindle fond memories of her first honeymoon by going on the cruise David had planned before his tragic accident. She confessed to Trevor that on various occasions during the trip she strayed from that intention. Even when she was able to envision being with David, the result was not always an affirming memory.

Trevor acknowledged his own guilt concerning Ava. As a foreign correspondent, she was gone so frequently that he eventually adjusted to being on his own. When Ava did show up for a few weeks, he regarded her presence as a disruption to his normal routine. Resentment displaced what should have been the joy of reunion.

Relieved to hear Trevor's disclosure, Sara acknowledged similar concerns over David's frequent fund-raising travels. "Even when David was home," she went on to say, "I knew his mind was elsewhere."

Trevor nodded in agreement and said something that caught Sara completely off-guard. "I learned that when someone's mind is elsewhere, so, too, is their heart in many cases."

Upon hearing this, Sara gulped and grew teary.

"I'm sorry, Sara. I've obviously upset you. I should keep my thoughts to myself."

"Please don't. Sometimes it's necessary to get upset in order to face the truth. That's what Simone would say, and I believe her."

After lunch Sara and Trevor purchased tickets to the castle grounds and strolled along the park's perimeter enjoying the beautiful views of Lisbon. For much of the time, they held hands. On the way back to the hotel, Sara admitted that her emotions were having a "vigorous workout" lately.

"I've gone from the unanticipated joy of hearing Simone sing to her unexpected death to an enchanting afternoon with you, Trevor. Such a roller coaster ride clearly betrays my given name. I believe a wee nap is in order before we go to dinner."

Trevor agreed that a nap sounded like a good idea. The two hugged, and Trevor left to catch tram twenty-eight back to his hotel.

Trevor and Jose arrived at the Hotel Pessoa a few minutes before eight. By that time a pelting rain was drenching Lisbon. Pastel joked about Simone having summoned the downpour with her rendition of "Stormy Weather" the previous evening. The limousine pulled up at eight, and the foursome got in.

When they reached Amalia's, Sara informed Domingo that Simone had passed away. He expressed genuine sorrow at the news and said he was honored that Simone spent her last night at his establishment. Before Luisa Gonsalves began her performance, Trevor bought a round of drinks for everyone in the restaurant and asked them to raise their glasses to a great lady.

When Luisa came to the stage, she acknowledged hearing of Simone's death and dedicated the first fado song to her memory.

EPILOGUE

The Lisbon authorities took eight days to release Simone's corpse for cremation. They contacted her lawyer in St. Louis, and he confirmed her plan to end her life in Lisbon and to be cremated there. The coroner ruled that Simone died of an overdose of oxycodone accompanied by alcohol.

Pastel returned to New York with her father and immediately began investigating graduate writing programs. The obituary she wrote for Simone was published by the St. Louis Post-Dispatch. Soon thereafter, the obituary editor for the newspaper contacted Pastel and told her that dozens of Simone's former students and colleagues read of her death and requested an in-depth article on her. He wondered if Pastel would be interested, and she agreed to prepare the article. Pastel let Sara know that she would send a copy of what she wrote to Amadou's sister in Rome.

Sara attended several of Jose's art classes as well as a studio session. At the studio session, the instructor invited Sara to participate in sketching a still life arrangement she created for her students. The instructor praised Sara's sketch and encouraged her to enroll in the graduate program in art for spring semester. Sara responded that she would love to participate if she could learn enough Portuguese to make it worthwhile. Jose offered his services as a language tutor and translator.

For the remainder of her time in Lisbon, Sara and Trevor were inseparable. They rented a car and visited the lovely village of Sintra. In Lisbon they explored the Gulbenkian Museum, the Art Museum of Dr. Anastacio Goncalves, the home of renowned fadista Amalia Rodrigues, Jeronimos Monastery, and the Ajuda National Palace. To say that Sara's love of art was reignited during this time would be a serious understatement.

Trevor located a funeral director and arranged for Simone's cremation. On a blustery fall morning, he and Sara carried the urn containing her ashes to the Belem Tower on the banks of the Tagus and cast them into the river. Sara read the words of "Stormy Weather" and expressed the hope that the souls of Simone and Amadou were now united.

Later that day, Sara emailed a lengthy message to Pastel telling her about Simone's cremation and her plans to study art in the spring in Lisbon. The email ended with an invitation for Pastel to join Sara's family and Trevor for Thanksgiving dinner in Charlottesville. Sara also reminded Pastel that she was welcome to stay with her if she decided to attend the University of Virginia's graduate writing program.

The day before flying back to the United States, Sara received a call from her daughter. Marie sounded uncharacteristically unsettled. She begged her mother to come to Charlotte and help care for Marcus while she and Parker searched for a house. Sara listened patiently before informing Marie that she had been invited to attend the University of Lisbon's art program.

"I'll be very busy in Charlottesville converting your old bedroom into an art studio, making arrangements for someone to look after the house in the spring, packing what I'll need in Portugal, and learning Portuguese. I'm afraid you'll need to hire an au pair or some local college student to help you with Marcus. I just can't deal with any more interruptions."

"I don't understand," Marie responded.

"One day when you're older, I'll explain. Please tell Marcus that Nana loves him and looks forward to seeing him for Thanksgiving."

On the plane ride back to Dulles International Airport, Sara decided to take out the sketch book that Jose had given her as a parting gift and sketch from memory Simone singing at Amalia's. When she reached into her travel bag, she noticed a white envelope in one of the side pockets. It was addressed to Marie. Sara had forgotten about the "just in case" letter she prepared before flying to Istanbul.

Slipping the envelop back into the pocket, she pulled out the sketch book and a pencil and began to visualize Simone's performance.

ABOUT THE AUTHOR

Daniel L. Duke got a late start writing novels, publishing his first book, *Man Camp*, at the tender age of seventy-five. Three additional novels followed in rapid succession: *River of Dreams*, *Pursuit of Happiness*, and now, *Serenity*. Born in Richmond, Virginia, Duke learned early on that the past is always present.

He majored in history at Yale and prepared to teach high school history. A job offer from Stanford University altered that careertrack and led to a dozen years on the Left Coast. Duke eventually found his way back to the Old Dominion as professor and department chair at Mr. Jefferson's university.

Among his thirty-five academic books were three major investigations of organizational history. The lure of fiction writing, however, could not be resisted when he retired. Duke lives near Charlottesville with Cheryl, his wife of forty-four years, and a bevy of beloved children and grandchildren.